MURDER ON THE GOLDEN HALO
AN EARTHLING MYSTERY
BY
W. H. BESWICK

AUTHOR'S NOTE

I am a princess. Please do not be impressed. On my planet alone, there are at least three hundred princesses, which does not count the ones claiming to be princesses. I am clueless as to why someone would make such a ridiculous claim. Considering the number of planets in the universe, there are billions of princesses.

Trust me. It is nothing to brag about.

I was just born into the right family. However, my father and mother would disagree. They are convinced I was switched at birth, but that is an entirely different story. Let us say I have chosen to live my life as I see fit, which, according to my mother, is not always acceptable behavior for a princess. If I lived the life my mother wanted, I would die of boredom. Not to mention, a princess has no privacy. From the day I was born, my life has been under a microscope. Then there are the arranged marriages. If you could have seen the prince, I was supposed to wed. Putting it tactfully, if he hadn't been a prince, he probably would have never been able to get married. Eventually, he married my sister, who was as thrilled as I was.

This produced a royal scandal, so thanks to my grandmother, who left me a considerable fortune, I could leave my world and see what the universe had to offer. Since I am twenty-first in line for the throne, I doubt I will ever be sitting on it. Honestly, my entire family was happy to see me go.

But not as happy as me. I will not miss the petticoats, corsets, slips, long gowns, and hair spray.

Now, this is my first book. I have been well educated—the one good thing about being a princess—and I love to read and did well in my writing classes. I had attempted to start books before but only got a few pages into them before I became bored with my words. I can only imagine how bored the reader would be.

So what happened to change things?

Well, murder.

A very important person was murdered on the very ship I was traveling on. I was right there in the thick of it all. It was exciting. How I ended up on the ship and who was murdered I will lay out in the following pages.

Now, gentle reader, you will note that the first few chapters are told in the third person. This is because I am recounting events where I was not present. The very same people involved retold these events to me. I took some liberties with the telling in some cases, but this was only for dramatic effect.

It is all true.

I also did this to inform the reader of the characters in this story. You must know who the players are in the play, so like any great director, I have set the stage.

Once the stage is set, I will tell the story from my point of view. You will see the events unfold as I saw them myself. At the end of my story, I pray your opinion of Earthlings will have changed.

Mine certainly did.

Oh, one last thing...no two. Some of the names have been changed, and you will note that I have written this in my native language but have used some universally understood words.

I pray you will enjoy this story. I will accept all praise, but please keep any derogatory comments to yourself.

Humbly yours,
Princess Deela

PROLOGUE

"Please come in."

"Ah, is there a problem? I...I...am going to be late for work."

"Do you know who I am?"

"Ah, yes. You are Lady Venusun from planet Sirona."

"What do you know about me?"

"You are tenth in line for the throne in your family. But you appear to have no interest in wearing the crown. Your interests are more in business and other world politics. You have been very successful in both of these pursuits. You are the head of over a dozen multi-planet corporations. The family fortune had conservatively grown..."

"Conservatively?"

"Ah, a poor word choice. The latest estimates suggest it has multiplied ten times. I can only guess since I can't access your private records. I know you have used this wealth to...well...ah...make yourself one of the most powerful females in ten sectors."

"More like twenty."

"I only have access to old newspapers and such, so the error in my speculation could lie there."

"Still. Quite impressive. How did you know?"

"Ah...oh, it was all just guesswork, my lady. It was a problem to work on to pass the time. I do enjoy a good puzzle."

"Murder is a puzzle to you?"

"I was once a police officer. Ah, ah, I could have been wrong."

"But you weren't. Explain."

"Well, Lady Venusun, aside from being rich and powerful, you are beautiful and still quite young regarding lifespans in your world. I suspected that although clever in manners in business and politics, you might be naïve when it comes to...ah...matters of the heart."

"Well, considering past events, I can't argue with you. Was that all?"

"Ah. Ah, no. Please don't be offended. I suspected you are used to getting what you want and only sometimes hear the word no. So this...well putting tactfully makes one...arrogant."

"Arrogant? Yes, you are quite right. I am more aware of that now. Thanks to you. Go on, give me more details. You interest me."

"Ah, I am not that interesting and really not as clever as you seem to believe."

"Enough with the...the...the. Whatever this is. Continue!"

"As you probably know, I work as a dishwasher at one of the most exclusive restaurants on this planet. I don't get out front for obvious reasons. But the rest of the staff tends to gossip."

"You listen to gossip?"

"Ah, ah, yes. Gossip can be very helpful in matters like this. The trick is listening to gossip, which is figuring out what is true and what is made up. There is always a bit of truth in gossip. People...all people, no matter the planet, love to gossip. Even the..."

"Yes, yes, go on."

"I was working the night the young lady came in and interrupted your meal. She made quite the scene. I could hear her back in the kitchen. From what I could hear and listen to the staff, I figured out that the young lady was the ex-lover of your new husband. They had been together for several years. The young lady was also a good friend of yours. A childhood friend. Unlike you, she had a title but no money. Your husband was in the same state before your marriage. Titled but poor. Because of this, your old friend came to you and asked you to employ her lover so they could be wed."

"I did. She was one of my best friends. I now know how poorly I treated her. What he lacked in money, he more than made up for in other ways. He was young, handsome, and clever. Very skilled in the bedroom. It wasn't just another...oh, what is the word I am looking for?"

"Affair?"

"Yes, an affair."

"But you fell in love with him."

"Yes, I fell in love with him."

"Yes, back on my world, it would be called a whirlwind romance. Everything seemed to be fine, aside from losing your friend. She vowed to make you both pay. While on your estate, you and your husband were beyond her reach."

"Then we went on what you called a honeymoon."

"Ah yes, it was on your honeymoon the trouble started. Your now ex-friend started to stalk you. For the last month, no matter where you went, she showed up and humiliated you in public. A scorned lover. Even made threats against your life."

"How did you figure out the plan was to murder me?"

"Ah, well, as I stated, you are wealthy, but your old friend was not. Yet, she was able to follow you to some of the most exclusive and private places on three planets. This was a woman who could barely pay her rent. Not only did she appear to travel in first class, but she was dressing quite fashionably. The question I asked myself was where she was getting the money. To follow you and your husband must have been very expensive."

"Which made you suspect my husband."

"Ah...my lady. Oh, yes, but more importantly, he gave her information on your travel plans. I watched your security, and they are excellent. Very smart and well trained. The fellow in charge is a very impressive man. Reminded me of my old Captain. He was also a smart man. They appeared to have several very clever ways to escape this young lady."

"Yet, she still found me."

"This was all guesswork. But I still felt your life might be in jeopardy."

"So you contacted my head of security, who, to their credit, took the time to listen to you. Because of this, they were able to thwart their plot. You suggested the attempt was going to be made on our next stop. They were going to shoot me while on a jungle cruise. Explain."

"Well, they knew that once you ended up dead, they would both be suspected. Your husband is charming and would easily deflect any questions of his innocence. The stalking was meant to draw attention away from him and to the young lady. So when you ended up dead, your husband would not be suspected. He would be looked upon as a victim. Of course, working together, I suspect they had worked out somehow to give the lady an alibi. An alibi that couldn't be questioned. I believe they picked the cruise on this world because...ah. How do I put this?"

"The local law enforcement is inexperienced when it comes to murder. I believe the last murder committed on this planet was over fifty years ago."

"Closer to fifty-five. The odds were in their favor, and the investigation would not be resolved. There might be gossip, but nothing that would put them in prison. After a year or two, they would have married."

"As they say on your world to live happily ever after..."

"Said on my world. Said my lady."

"Yes, you are quite right. Suggesting my people watch my husband and cabin not only saved my life but put both of them behind bars. The prisons here are quite deplorable. I think in time, I will arrange the release of my friend. My actions were wrong. As for my husband, he can rot."

"Ah, if that is all, my lady, I must get to work. I am already late."

"Stop worrying about dirty dishes. Your talents are wasted in the kitchen. I do understand why you were forced to take such a disparaging job. No, no, I could use someone like you. I want you to work for me."

"As what, my lady?"

"Problem solver. I have a few problems that I am sure you can solve for me."

"I thank you for the offer, but I don't think your head of security would......approve."

"Oh, he agrees with me. Like me, he respects intelligence. No matter who has it? We both think you will be quite helpful to both of us."

CHAPTER 1

THE GOLDEN HALO

The Golden Halo is a privately owned ship. Lady Venusun built it to make deep space travel less tedious and much more comfortable.

The comforts and services were outstanding for those who could afford the fare. Even the service for those who couldn't afford the royal deck was quite good.

At least, that is what I have been told.

It is considered one of the most beautiful spaceships in many sectors. Its gold and black exterior, along with its webbed fins on the sides and back, gives it the appearance of a majestic bird flying through the stars.

The ship has seven levels. The lowest level is for baggage and other items too big to fit in one's cabin. The level just above this one is for the kitchens, crew quarters, supplies, and luggage compartments. Ten staircases and eight elevators give the crew easy and quick access to the passengers above.

The two lowest levels contain smaller cabins. There is more than one room with a cot, and the bathroom is so tiny you can barely turn around. They all dine together in banquet halls on cuisine that is, well, for lack of a better word, common. Naturally, these are occupied by people with limited resources.

The next level is a step up in quality, catering to wealthy tourists and businessmen. The dining rooms were quite good. There are two theaters, a small casino, and several small bars.

The sixth level is usually occupied by the staff of the passengers on the royal level—servants, aides, bodyguards, and such. Those who weren't quite rich enough to afford the royal level took up the rest of the cabins.

The royal level is taken up by one main casino offering all games of chance and a full bar staffed with a hostess to ensure everyone is having a good time. There were smaller game rooms, but these were usually reserved for private parties. Across from the casino was a restaurant with a gourmet chef. The décor is done to reflect that of an old sailing vessel. Further down is the gym/spa, complete with a pool. Membership required. There was a public pool for those lacking membership, but no one used it.

The rich and powerful don't bathe with persons they don't know.

Several small cafés also offer dishes from many different worlds. Naturally, the menu is quite pricey.

There was also a food court, which offered dishes at very reasonable prices. This was mainly to cater to the staff from the lower level. There were three theaters: two for movies and the last for live performances.

There were only three ways to access the royal level. The only way was through an elevator manned by an armed guard. The code to operate the doors was known only to him and changed daily.

New day. New code.

This security was because the luxury cabins took up the entire floor. All are staterooms and have a parlor, bedroom, and full bath. Two of the cabins had two bedrooms. Each cabin gave the passenger a fantastic view of the stars and planets through large windows. Some cabins have thick red plush carpets with dark wood walls and brass fittings, once again representing an old sailing vessel. The furnishings have a definite masculine feel. Others are decorated with bright pastels and overstuffed furniture with a female's taste in mind. All are decorated to give the guest the most comfort possible.

The other two ways to access the royal level are by staircases, which are only to be used by the crew of the Golden Halo. A key is required to access the staircases, which are also guarded.

No one had access to the bridge except for the bridge crew. This rested on the front of the ship above the royal level. The Captain and his executive officers have their quarters from the bridge. An elevator ran directly from the lowest level to the bridge. This, too, was coded and guarded. The engineering stations, maintenance, and the galley for the crew are built into the rear lower section of the Golden Halo. There is only one door to these areas. Like the other doors, one needed an access code to gain entrance.

The whole design of the ship kept the crew and passengers separated, except for the hostesses, maids, valets, and entertainers. Only these and the high-ranking officers had contact with passengers.

Only the very rich can afford to be on the seventh level of the Golden Halo. On this particular voyage, several cabins were reserved for the wedding party of Queen Rexannis Windsax of the planet Icakka.

CHAPTER 2

QUEEN REXANNIS WINDSAX

The youngest and perhaps one of the most beautiful queens to have ever come to the throne was Queen Rexannis Windsax. The young Queen stood a little over six feet tall for a woman on her world. Her father had been tall, and her mother beautiful. She benefited from both their genes. Her face is oval-shaped, with a soft chin and sharp cheekbones. The large green eyes were rare in her world. They were not only beautiful but suggested a shrew mind. Her figure was slender for her world but would have been considered voluptuous on other worlds. Windsax's long hair was a waterfall of tight green curls that fell to her knees. It was rarely seen down. As a princess and Queen, she always styled her hair into elaborate twists and buns. Her skin was also green but a much lighter shade than her hair. As was tradition, she wore a long, flowing white silk gown with gold trim. It fell to her ankles, but one slit hinted at a long shapely leg. She wore no crown or jewelry of any kind. This was also custom. In her world, a soon-to-be-married woman went to the altar only adorned with her beauty and purity.

Queen Windsax stood at the window of her suite, watching the vast landscape of stars and planets before her. The universe was so extensive that it made her feel so small, a rare thing for a queen. There were times she wished she could be like her friend Princess Deela.

Young and free.

But she was a queen. Not just by birthright but by choice. A choice that no one knew she had made. It was the first life-changing decision she had made.

Her older brother was heir to the throne. From the day he was born, he was groomed and trained for this. But all the grooming and training cannot truly change what is inside. The prince was selfish and so very arrogant. To add to that, he was a fool. Her father and mother realized this. The throne was his by blood and birth. They were considering changing tradition and appointing Rexannis as heir. The senate and temple leaders secretly agreed with this. For they, too, knew a fool when they saw one.

Before the announcement could be made, both of her parents died tragically in a shuttle crash. While it was still under investigation, the prince attempted to take the throne even though he knew it was against his parents' wishes. A long, bitter struggle was avoided when the prince died from a virus.

At least, that is what all the reports said.

Princess Rexannis Windsax suspected her brother and his followers had a hand in her parents' death. She had no proof, but sure, as there were twelve Gods, he had a hand in the murder of their parents. Everyone seemed to ignore the fact the princess had studied medicine and chemistry. Everyone except her brother's friends and followers wanted to put this behind them. They complained until the crown rested upon her head. Then, for their own well-being, they closed their lips.

In Windsax's mind, she did no wrong. The crown was meant to be hers. She was destined to be Queen. A queen must be ready to do whatever is needed to protect the throne and her people. A queen must make the hard choices.

Now, another decision had to be made.

Her fiancé was older by ten years. Although not of royal blood, he came from one of the oldest and most respected families. The Prime Centurion Bacco Uxtel had served with honor and incredible bravery in the Earth Wars. He was the perfect match, made better by the fact she loved him. At least she did before the wars. Like everyone, the Earth Wars had changed him.

The green eyes closed.

Time for another choice.

CHAPTER 3

PRIME CENTURION BACCO UXTEL

Bacco Uxtel stood in the bathroom, studying his face. It was a face new to him. The surgeon had done excellent work, but there were still scars. There were more scars on his body—lifetime memories of the wars. The Prime Centurion was tired of fighting. He was pondering his future.

"A new face. A new life." He mused to himself.

His mind drifted to Queen Rexannis. She was indeed a beautiful woman, with a beauty that could make any man feel like a fool. Then she would speak, revealing the keen, sharp mind behind those green eyes. Sometimes, he felt like a child in her presence.

Well, she was a queen. He would never be king. He would be a prince in name, even if the Queen died.

Bacco Uxtel pushed this thought aside. It was best not to have such thoughts. It was a bad omen. His dark blue eyes drifted over his broad, muscular body. The scars criss-crossed his chest. His hair had started falling out before the Earth Wars. Now, he just shaved his head. Being from the high mountains, his skin was pale and almost white. Some said it nearly looked like the untanned Earthlings' flesh. He shook his head. Some fools still thought Earthlings came in one color.

"Sir, are you all right?"

His friend Zana asked through the closed door. He glanced back. Then, he looked down at his hand. It was shaking. He grabbed the quivering thing with his other hand. He had to keep it together. He had been brave in battle. Now, he must be more fearless than he ever had. "I am fine. I am just moving a little slowly. We must dress for dinner."

CHAPTER 4

BETA CHIEF ZANA

Beta Chief Zana was short for his kind and a bit too soft around the middle. His taste for rich food was the reason for this. Rather than exercise, he had chosen to let out all his uniforms. His daily attire was a black jacket and pants with gold trim on the sleeves and down the side of the pant legs. The shirt was white with gold buttons. His bow tie and vest were purple. Like the Prime Centurion, he was bald. But this was by choice. Unlike his widening body, his face was narrow, and he had a pointed chin, which gave him an odd appearance. His eyes were small and a dull brown. His skin was darker than his master's, but not by much. The color of his brown eyes and skin seemed to let everyone know he had risen, some would say, above his stage in life.

From a very young age, his life had been in the military. There were few opportunities in the small town he was born. He joined to escape the city and see the universe. As he rose through the ranks, he saw the many worlds. Sadly, they rarely visit what would be called tourist sites. Then came the Earth Wars. Thanks to this, he now saw worlds ravaged, not just by the wars but by the Earthlings, who had come out into the universe like it belonged to them. There were rumors the Earthlings had ravaged and pillaged their own world, bringing it almost to extinction.

Perhaps that would have been better.

Rather than repair the damage to their own world, they came out into the universe, apparently thinking...like ripe fruit, the universe was theirs for the taking.

Business as usual.

They had been wrong. It took time, but the universe fought back.

The wars lasted too long. Far too many died. Whole worlds were almost destroyed. For what? The greed of the Earthlings.

Zana felt his anger growing but stopped himself. The wars were over. It was time to move on, heal, and rebuild the universe.

During the wars, he had been placed under the command of one of the bravest soldiers he had met. Soon, he came to be more than another officer. They became friends. After the war, he stayed with the Prime Centurion. They had fought side by side in the war. Now they would...would what? Put everything behind them. Everything that happened in the war. Could they really do that? Could they really put all the pain and suffering behind them? Forget all the comrades and family that had been lost in the war.

They must put the horrors of war behind them for the greater good.

CHAPTER 5

DOCTOR ALLTON CRAG

There was a time when Dr. Allton Crag was one of the most brilliant surgeons in the world. The words gifted, clever, and even genius had been used to describe him. He had not objected. Allton had been younger and very conceited. Before the mistake, he had been considered a genius. His patients had been some of the wealthiest and most powerful on his world.

It hadn't even been a huge mistake. It was a mistake that could have been fixed. The patient just had to give Allton a chance to fix it. Sadly, the mistake had been made by someone with wealth and connections. Then, the rumors of his drinking came out. Unspoken accusations that he may have been drunk. It matters not whether the rumors were true. His life was left in ruins in less time than he could have imagined. Leaving his world didn't help. The rumors followed him. The great genius was now a ship's doctor. It wasn't a bad job. It was a luxury ship. The food was well prepared. He was treated respectfully but wasn't in the operating room. Most of his cases dealt with space sickness, food poisoning, and other minor complaints.

He missed the lights and accolades.

Allton had even looked the part with his tall, lean body and face, not handsome but wise. His skin was a pleasant blue with purple stripes on his cheeks and arms. His once full, rich purple hair had thinned or fallen out, leaving the top of his head bald. His past patients had looked into his violet eyes and believed he could do miracles. He believed, too. He didn't think he had a drinking problem.

He was a doctor. He would know.

The doctor adjusted his short white dinner jacket with some symbols on the shoulders denoting his rank. It wasn't custom-made, but it fit well enough. He had seen a picture of an Earthling in the same outfit. The Earthlings did know a thing or two about fashion. The white jacket went well with his light blue skin.

His cold blue eyes studied his reflection in the mirror. Dinner at the Captain's table. He had dined there before but never with a queen. This wouldn't be his first time meeting Queen Rexannis, but it would be the first time since the army hospital. Back then, he had been the man who saved the man she had loved her entire life. She had been quite gracious and even gave him a lovely gift, which he sold.

The doctor looked down at his shaking hand. He needed to be careful. No wine, or just one glass. If he played his part well, he would soon be back in the limelight.

CHAPTER 6

THE PRIME MINISTER

Ley Tunga was the youngest prime minister on her home world. This had been achieved not by being born into the right family. She had no only title or money. She was also very bright and ambitious. The fact that she was also beautiful had been another factor.

The young alien beauty had the same shade of skin as Queen Rexannis. She was shorter and had a fuller body, which seemed to appeal to all males regardless of what planet they came from. Ley wore dresses to accent her lovely curves, but not too much. She was, after all, the prime minister. Her green hair fell into tight curls to her shoulders. She had an oval face with full lips and hazel eyes that were just as rare as green. Her beauty had been an asset, but not in the way one would think. They saw the pretty face and assumed there was nothing inside her head. Happily, those days were behind her. Ley now had a reputation for being cold and brilliant. Many even questioned her marriage. Was it really for love or just another power move? Eyebrows were raised, and tongues wagged when her husband died. A boating accident. The body was never found. It was sad that he had survived the war to then die so tragically.

Let them talk. Ley was now the second most powerful woman in her world.

Ley tried her third outfit before sitting at the Captain's table. She wasn't trying to impress the Captain. She was trying to impress upon her Queen that not all her subjects groveled and whimpered in her presence. The prime minister was part of a growing movement that felt the royals had outlived their purpose. Ley, her cabinet, and the Senate ran the government, but then Queen Rexannis had a tight grip on the reins of power. Everything could only be done with her approval. Even though Ley had been elected, the Queen could remove her with a word. In her opinion, a queen should have been nothing more than a figurehead. Sadly, the Queen was a well-loved figurehead. There would be riots in the streets if they attempted to overthrow the Queen.

Heads would literally roll.

A revolt was made even more impossible when the Queen, with her royal inspectors, exposed all the corruption in the very government Ley had set up. She lost many allies and some friends but held on to her position.

But for how long?

It was apparent that Queen Rexannis wanted to streamline the bureaucracy. She argued that this would cut down on corruption. She was right, but this would also give Her Majesty most of the power.

This was unacceptable.

The young prime minister had come too far to be cast aside on a queen's whim.

Ley couldn't help but think about her world's unique situation. They had a queen with no heirs. A plane crash had seen to that. A plane the Queen was supposed to be on. At the last minute, she changed her mind. A whim that saved the Queen's life.

The prime minister knew something had to be done before the wedding. The wedding could occur, but the ceremony could not, not the wedding night.

If the Queen were to die. There would be no one to inherit the throne. The public would accept a queen dying off. No heir. No queen. They could make a clean break from this foolish and very expensive tradition.

Well, not every ruler wore a crown.

"If I have the courage, I will make history," Ley said, talking to her reflection in the mirror. "It will be so easy. Of course, there is the Prime Centurion. No, he won't be a problem. Focus on the Queen. You can do this."

CHAPTER 7

ENSIGN YULA SIG

Ensign Yula Sig was confused. The young officer was in her small cabin, thinking about her conversation with the Captain.

Some passengers were going to play poker. It was a private game—not unusual—held on the Royal level in one of the executive suites. Still, it was not unusual. They needed a dealer—of course, they did. One of the players had requested her to be the dealer.

There were others whose job it was to run the games. All were trained to play the game, even the Earth game poker. Granted, back in college, before the war, she had worked in a casino as a card dealer, so she knew the game, but why would someone from the royal level want her to deal? The Captain had come to her cabin and told her about the request. Then, I asked her the same question that was bouncing around in her head.

Why?

Yula looked at her reflection in the mirror. She was not unattractive or ugly. She had one of those nondescript faces that usually went unnoticed. Her figure was slender, and she had just a little fat around her belly. Pointed ears pushed through her brown hair, which she kept cut short. All in all, Ensign Yula Sig was unremarkable.

Which was how she liked it. She wanted to go through life unnoticed. Yula had joined the service when the war broke out. Like many, she had fought bravely and been awarded medals. After the war, she resigned her commission. It had been time to move on. She applied for jobs on luxury spaceships. The plan had been to get a position and work on a ship for as long as she could. Hopefully, until she retired. By then, the war would be just a distant memory.

Which was fine with her.

She remembered her mother's advice. Keep your wits about you and your head down.

CHAPTER 8

ZUMO ZECKE

Zumo Zecke, not his real name, sat in his suite watching the stars and planets. He enjoyed watching the universe. It was so peaceful. It made one reflect on one's life. His home planet had been small. It was a nice, tranquil place. A place he had no interest in leaving. It wasn't until the war he was forced to leave. His first taste of traveling. If you called moving from planet to planet to fight the Earthlings traveling. No more long walks through quiet streets or enjoying art in a gallery back home. Landing in some cities that, in some cases, were nothing more than crumbled ruins. Before the war he had been in college. Two years in, he still didn't know what he wanted to study. He had been leaning toward something in numbers. An accountant. A nice, quiet job that he could do alone. His girlfriend approved of this plan.

Then the war came.

He was drafted and made an officer. It was during his first year that the absolute horror of war hit him. His girlfriend had been killed in an attack. His hatred for the Earthlings burned like fire. He vowed to make them pay. Once the laid-back officer, he became a true leader to his men. His superiors saw his rage and put it to good use. He was given promotions and medals. They meant nothing to him. Then they moved him into more interesting work for which he surprisingly had a talent.

At first, all that mattered was that the Earthlings would pay—not just for the death of his love but for taking away the quiet life he had dreamed of. Then something changed. Maybe he saw that both sides were capable of terrible things. His thirst for revenge faded. His attitude was that the Earthlings were no worse than anyone else.

By the war's end, he had a skill set that was not very practical in day-to-day life. He was offered a position in an agency that handled secret and delicate matters. It was one of those agencies people hoped didn't exist but inwardly knew they did. Shadow agencies sometimes did questionable things that could be considered illegal or immoral.

He learned the horrible truth he had come to suspect. The rich and powerful went from all planets and used the war to increase their wealth and power.

Now, his new job was much more complicated and difficult. Secrecy was paramount. His latest targets were strangers who had supposedly done terrible things. Sometimes, no reason was given. It was during his time working for this agency he realized he had lost his conscious. After this, he decided to go freelance. His employers had no problem with that. Just as long as his services were available to them.

Now, these talents were available to everyone who had money.

Zumo was now a killer. He could have used the term assassin, but he felt that calling himself a killer was being honest with himself. He did kill people. The quiet little man had a talent for it.

Zumo stood barely five feet. His frame was thin. Some said it was too thin. He had a skinny body with a dull skin tone and a face that could be mistaken for a being from one of a dozen planets. His hair was brown. Just brown. Few people knew how dangerous he was. The thin arms and legs were pure muscle. He was trained in several fighting skills. Zumo rarely used these skills. A pistol sometimes or a sniper's rifle was his preference. A quick shove down a staircase was always good. Poison was the best. No one asked questions.

The alien had been booked under the false name. He was supposedly a successful professional. A professional what? No one asked. Zumo had been booked at a level just below the Royal Level.

This was a problem.

This meant sneaking up to the Royal Level to reach his target. Actually, there were two targets, but the second one was optional. The main target must be taken out first. Getting to the primary target had been impossible, but he heard about the game. He would never be invited to the game.

Zumo didn't understand poker. If he had put his mind to it, he could have understood the game, but he had no time for games. The killer just needed to get close to his target—the biggest target of his life. If he completed this job, he could retire. But then what?

CHAPTER 9

TITALUS

Titalus was his real name but not the name he was using now. The name Daris was the name he took during and after the war. It had been necessary for his survival. Before the war, he had a life. A simple life. He had owned a small factory.

He had been happy.

Then, the Earthlings came to his world.

Very friendly at first, using words like peace and love. Now he knew these were just words. Looking back, he realized how easily he had been seduced by their words and promises. Promises of wealth and power. All he had to do was betray his people.

The Earth woman who made these promises had been so beautiful. Yes, now he knew she had just seduced him.

At least, that was what he told himself. It made his past actions seem right.

At first, it had been nothing more than shuffling pages and keeping all the accounts in order. Titalus watched as the Earthlings started to use the courts of his world, with the government's help, to steal the lands of people, some of whom had been his friends. Naturally, his people began to object.

That was when the soldiers came. No need to be subtle any longer. Weapons were used to take what they wanted. The Earthlings wanted everything, and he helped. It was surprising how fast they took control of his world. He now knew they had it down to an art.

He watched as the Earthlings used their machines to ravage the once-beautiful lands. They polluted the rivers and seas. The skies became dark, and the smell of death lingered in the air.

Titalus turned a blind eye to it all. He now had more money than he could ever spend in his lifetime. The beautiful Earthling was now his wife. He had a large house and more. He was thrilled when his mistress announced she was pregnant.

Life seemed to be perfect.

For so many good years, he lived this life. A beautiful wife and child.

It ended so quickly.

The arrogance of the Earthlings had been their undoing. They had assumed other worlds would just accept their ways. They had been wrong.

So wrong.

So had he.

Titalus had started to hear rumors of rebellions on other worlds. On some worlds, there appeared to be an all-out war. Wars that the Earthlings were losing. The news agencies in his world played down all these stories, calling them false.

Of course, by this time, the Earthlings controlled what the public saw and heard.

Then, one night, the combined forces of other planets invaded his world with the help of the underground. The underground that Earthlings and many like him had thought was just an annoyance had actually been laying the groundwork for the invasion. In mere days, the Earthlings began to flee. His wife fled to Earth with their child. He had promised he would join her there.

He had no intention of going to Earth.

He knew his name would come up as a criminal. With his ill-gotten gains, he fled the only home he had known. He took on the new name, hiding his wealth in accounts spread around several worlds. To complete his cover, he even joined the fight against the Earthlings.

After the war, his real name was still on the list of traitors. Thankfully, he was low on the list, but he knew it was only a matter of time before he would be on top of the list. During the war, he found a disgraced surgeon to give him a new face. When he looked in the mirror, he saw almost a complete stranger. There were still traces of his old face and pointed ears. It would be enough. Most of his close friends had been killed. His wife and child had been on the Earth.

Or so he thought.

The first bad news was his ill-gotten wealth had been found. Now almost penniless, he fled.

He kept moving from place to place. Somehow, he knew one day they would catch up with him. The man known as Titalus had done some terrible things. His dead wife had spoken about something called karma.

Now, it seemed this day may have come. It was like his past had come to him and said remember me. A face from the past. He almost fainted but realized the other person hadn't recognized him. It was for this reason he stayed in his cabin. The plan was to stay in the cabin until the invitation to play poker with Prime Centurion Bacco Uxtel came.

Titalus had served under the Prime Centurion. The invitation made it clear he couldn't say no. He knew that Bacco didn't just want to see an old army buddy. The older alien told himself to calm down. If the Prime Centurion wanted to expose him, he could have done it long ago. Of course, Daris knew things, too. Things that powerful people didn't want to know.

He was so tired of moving—always moving. He could end this nomadic life. He just had to wait and see what the Prime Centurion wanted.

CHAPTER 10

PRINCESS DEELA

Well, you have met the major players in this story. There are some minor players, but these are the important ones. Before I continue, I should tell you a little more about myself. As I mentioned, I am a princess.

Not a very good one.

I choose, as the Earthlings say, to walk my own path. I do wear long, beautiful gowns from time to time. When the situation calls for it. My preferred outfits will shock you to no end. I like specific Earth fashion. I love their blouses, things they call tee-shirts, and the pants they call jeans, but they have to be washed numerous times to get them the right color and softness. The best thing the Earthlings came up with were things called sneakers. These, without a doubt, are the most comfortable shoes in the universe. Especially the ones called Nike, Adidas, Reebok, Vans, and my favorite, Converse high tops. The Converse comes in various colors, but I like black and white. Thankfully, being a princess and being rich has helped fill my closets with enough pairs to last me a lifetime. How I obtained all these items was not entirely legal. If I was not a princess, questions would be asked.

I am considered beautiful, and I find no reason to disagree. I stand about six feet tall and have a perfect figure that does turn heads, especially when I wear something tight and short. I wear pink hair in an Earth style called a pageboy. It falls just above my shoulders. I also have pink eyes and freckles on my pale skin that refuse to tan. I really want a golden tan like I see in the pictures of Earth women. Apparently, it will not happen.

As you can tell, I am fascinated with the Earth and its culture. I am one of the few beings who think not all Earthlings are ruthless, greedy killers, which is another reason my family was thrilled to see me leave my home world.

An Earth-loving princess who talks about them and is a literal walking fashion statement for them was seen as embarrassing.

I booked passage on the Golden Halo, unaware that Queen Rexannis was on board. I do know her. She is one of the few royal bloods I know and actually like. As I pointed out, millions, probably billions, of beings claim to have royal blood. All these royal bloods have the same arrogant attitude and believe they are better than the common folk.

Back to my story, I was making my way to the pleasure planet Tridase. I had heard an actual Earthling had been there. Unsurprisingly, I have never seen an Earthling in the flesh. Oh, I have seen pictures.

It is not the same.

It was supposed to be a quick flight to the Tridase, but then Rexannis came aboard, and now we are making a side trip so she can get married. This means another two weeks on the Golden Halo.

Most annoying.

But that's the royals for you.

The only good news was that Prime Centurion Bacco Uxtel was on board. This was good news indeed. I had a score to settle with the Prime Centurion.

CHAPTER 11

There are a few obligations demanded of one of royal blood that I do abide by, such as when the Captain of the vessel invites you to sit at his table. You accept.

Which is how I ended up sitting at Captain Fross' table. I don't know the man, but he does seem to fidget a lot, which should concern me since he is in charge of the ship. He is a small, roundish fellow with hair and a beard that were a bit black for my taste. I suspect the good Captain's hair color comes from a bottle. His black uniform with all the brass buttons and gold trim had been tailored to fit his oval body. He should have hired a better tailor. Of course, it didn't help; his legs and arms seemed too short for his body. He did have bright yellow eyes that seemed to shine, but there was also a sadness in them. Fross seemed very good at being polite and acting interested in whoever was talking to him.

A necessary skill not only for captains but for princesses, too.

The ship captain sat by the Queen herself. She was indeed more beautiful than the last time I saw her. You never can tell with photo images. So much can be done with computers and lighting. She was wearing a very simple white gown with a gold tiara to hold back two long curls from her face. The rest was pinned up into a style that was defying gravity.

Kudos to her maid.

With hair that long, she must spend hours in the shower, washing it, and combing it out.

Or she has servants to do that.

Beside her was the man she loved, Prime Centurion Bacco Uxtel. He wore a white uniform without medals, ribbons, or any usual decorations officers wore.

I found it amusing that they were both wearing white. A sign of their chastity. Going to the altar, pure as snow. Trust me. If those two are virgins, I am not a princess.

I was slightly annoyed because Uxtel ignored me, or maybe it was the scars. I had heard he had been wounded in the war. Almost killed. It wasn't the face I remembered, but it was close enough. I assumed the General had gotten the best medical treatment money could buy. Whoever worked on him earned his money. Being at the other end of the table made it almost impossible to have a chat with him.

Oh, did I forget to tell you? I knew the prime centurion before the war. We met in a casino of all places. Uxtel was playing poker and getting disgusted with the other players. Poker isn't really about luck. There are a lot of skills in the game. Bluffing means knowing when to fold when to raise, and when to get up and walk away. The other players couldn't bluff if their lives depended on it. I could read their tells from across the room. The prime centurion was about to leave when I stepped up and challenged him. At first, he laughed and started to walk away.

The word coward made him stop and look back. It was then he saw I was serious. He made some clever remarks about how he should charge me for the lessons he was about to give me.

Lessons indeed.

We played well into the night. Uxtel won in the end, but I came out on top the next night. By the end of the week, he had won the last hand. We shared a meal and a drink and parted good friends. His being on the ship was, I took, a fortuitous encounter to get some payback. Bacco was one of the best poker players I knew.

But so far, his attention had been divided between his fiancé, the Captain, and another younger man in a blue dress uniform. He had all the usual decorations so the world would know what a good little soldier he was. He was pale and bald, just like the General. My keen eye told me he had some surgery done. Wars will leave scars.

The lady sitting next to me was the prime minister of the Queen's world. Ley Tunga was beautiful, with a bosom that kept threatening to spill out of her dress, which was too tight. I can only imagine it was these assets that got her elected. She kept on trying to drag me into a discussion on politics. I do not discuss politics or religion with anyone. It is a surefire way to start a debate that usually ends in an argument. No one walks away happy. Not to mention what it does to one's digestion.

Besides, politics bores me, and religion interests me even less. One day, I will have to answer for my lack of faith, but not today. Today, the wine was good, and so was the meal.

Across from me was the ship's doctor. A tall, slender man with an intelligent face. The color of his skin and stripes told what planet he was from. His name was Allton Crag. I knew the name and the man by the scandal. How the mighty had fallen. He was wearing a very white uniform jacket that looked almost new. It showed no signs of wear and tear. The good doctor either cared for his clothes, or they were new to him. Considering his reputation, I didn't only wonder how he got to be the ship's doctor but also how he was sitting at the Captain's table. I did notice he was on his second glass of wine.

Nervous?

Maybe not.

I was hoping something would happen. Space voyages are tedious, and a nice conflict makes things more interesting.

The last person at the table was a young ship's officer—an ensign, I think. By the look on her face and her nervously looking around or showing too much interest in her food, this young lady was either not used to being at the Captain's table, or was it all this royalty? I found her nervousness and pointed ears interesting. As an excellent poker player, I knew something was going on here.

I thought of an excellent Earth murder mystery novel I had read. The dapper detective always talked about putting the little gray cells to work.

I think I will do just that.

CHAPTER 12

THE EARTHLING PROBLEM

"Are you telling me you actually favor this proposal?"

Dr. Crag was speaking to the Prime Centurion. The question came out of nowhere. Bacco stopped bringing the glass of wine to his lips. The Prime Centurion looked genuinely surprised. He leaned forward. The doctor continued. "The Earthlings are savages. The universe is still recovering from the wars that they started."

"I am afraid the Prime Centurion is quite pro-earthling," Ley said, putting her elbows on the table. Had the woman been brought up in a barn? Still, she looked excited. She was finally getting the discussion she wanted. "Which I find fascinating since he had been on the front line. He better than anyone knows what Earthlings are capable of."

"As I have pointed out to you before, Prime Minister. Not all Earthlings are alike. Most of them are just like us." Bacco said with no hint of embarrassment. Considering his face, you would think he would be more...oh, what is the word I am looking for?

Resentful?

Hostile?

Oh, bother, I'll come back to it.

The general continued. "During the war, I interacted with many of the Earthlings. Prisoners of war and such. Most had no idea why they were fighting this war. Many had been forced to enlist. Even more were wondering why more efforts weren't being put into peace talks."

"They had no interest in talking peace," Crag said, then gulped down his wine. He actually wiped his mouth on his sleeve. "They came out into space and acted like it was their right to ravage and pillage. Entire populations were enslaved. Some planets are polluted so badly that it will take years for their recovery. Savages."

"My dear sir," Queen Rexannis said with a soft but firm voice with just the hint of a smile on her lips. "Are you suggesting we were not already polluting our own worlds? The Lacarty were already enslaved. Several planets were already at war."

"This diversity enabled the Earthlings to get as far as they did." Prime Centurion Uxtel said, leaning forward but not putting his elbows on the table. "The one positive thing that wars brought about was the Unification of Planets. Now, instead of fighting among ourselves, we talk."

"I find that surprising." Ensign Sig said, finally looking up from her plate. The nervousness was suddenly gone. She was looking right into the Prime Centurion's face. "You are a soldier. If memory serves me right, you were part of the final act."

"Yes, I was there when the final act was presented," he said, looking at the young officer with an odd expression. I was opposed to the final act. Sadly, I was not one of the twenty to make the final decision."

I noted that the Prime Centurion glanced at the prime minister

"Genocide is never the solution. It is morally wrong. We attempted to wipe out an entire race. Thank the Gods, we failed."

"Happily, there are still some around," I said with a smile. This got me some cool glares, but I ignored them. "They must have some virtues. Look at their fashion, and I understand Earth cuisine is quite delicious."

"Oh, you are right on that account." Optio Zana said with a smile and nod. "I had what they call a hamburger. It was messy but quite tasty. I believe the General has tasted something called Chinese food."

"Oh yes, I think it was called Kung Pao Beef. Very spicy, served over rice." Uxtel said with a nod as if remembering the tasty dish. "But the fact is, thanks to us, just a few thousand Earthlings are left. Even after the war, they were being hunted down and killed. Thank the Gods we put a stop to that."

"By executing some of our own!" Prime Minister Tunga snapped, banging her hand on the table. "Was that really necessary?"

"Yes!" The Prime Centurion growled, looking quite angry. The war had changed him. The Bacco I knew was very slow to anger. "The war was over. They had surrendered. What those people were doing was murder. Nothing more than cold-blooded murder. Hangings dragged behind cars, stoned, and worse. Wasn't it enough we turned their planet into a scorched ball where nothing will be able to live for centuries!? The final act affects not only soldiers but also women and children. It killed...no, murdered everything. We went too far. There was no honor in this victory. We owe them a new home."

"Well, you may be right," Ley muttered, but I suspected she disagreed. I suspected she realized she was upsetting the Prime Centurion, and considering he was about to marry a queen, it was the smart thing to do.

"So, are they any closer to finding a home for the Earthlings?" I asked.

"Actually, the commission hasn't even started to look." Queen Rexannis said in a calm voice that suggested her disgust with the lack of progress. "Many still share the same view as our prime minister."

These last words were directed right at the lady beside me. Ley Tunga attempted to stare the Queen down but lost.

"Even after we get approval," Prime Centurion Uxtel said grimly. There is the problem of the Earthlings being scattered around on goodness knows how many planets."

"It is my understanding Lady Venusun has one on her staff," Rexannis said. "Some kind of consular, I think?"

"What?" I gasped. "Lady Venusun employs an Earthling? I knew there was a reason I liked her. What do you know about him?"

The Queen smiled brightly. She seemed thrilled to be able to move on to another topic. "I know he supposedly saved her life."

CHAPTER 13

THE EARTHLING

"An Earthling saved her life?' I said with genuine surprise. This went against everything I had known about Earthlings. Indeed, I have never met one, but I have done my research. The men were all very strong, most having tattoos on their arms and sometimes on their chests and backs. They wore leather jackets and jeans, along with sneakers or boots. They would do almost anything while puffing on a cigar. Apparently, they were excellent lovers. The women were supposed to be very beautiful and seductive. My dear mother had warned me not to leave anyone I cared about alone with an Earthling. "How did he do this?"

Images of a huge, muscle-bound Earthling rushing to save the powerful lady filled my head. A gun in hand, blazing away.

"You must have heard about Lady Venusun's marriage to that penniless commoner."

"Well, he was penniless but very handsome."

"Turned out her pretty new husband was plotting her murder with the help of his old lover," Rexannis said in a hushed tone, suggesting it was a well-kept secret. Still, everyone at the table could hear her. "Somehow, the Earthling figured out the plot and saved her. Both ended up in prison."

"Actually, I believe the woman has been released," Bacco said with a sniff. "One year in prison. Lady Venusun felt she had caused the problem by stealing her oldest friend's lover."

"It is a perfect lesson or perhaps warning," Roxanne said with a smile before sipping some wine. "Be careful who you fall in love with. You may find more pain and suffering than love."

"Should I be concerned?" The Prime Centurion playfully asked, squeezing her hand at the same time.

"No, my darling, you give me nothing but joy."

I do not believe in love, perhaps because I have yet to fall in love. On the other hand, the Queen and Prime Centurion seemed to be very much in love. Falling in love is like playing poker. You can win some hands and lose others, but only when the last card is turned over do you know if you have won.

You think me heartless for this?

My mother thinks I am young and foolish.

It could be in matters of the heart.

"It is my understanding he has been quite helpful to her." Beta Chief Zana said with a nod. "Mind you, this could just be gossip. But he found out Countess Karo's husband had stolen some emeralds to pay off some debts. He recovered some pearls for another lady. There are even rumors he solved a few murders."

"We would have heard of this," I said, feeling a little insulted. An Earthling solving murders would be on all the news sites. I searched websites for stories about Earthlings. "It has to be gossip."

"It is my understanding he lets the local law enforcement take full credit," Zana continued. He is keeping a low profile, which shows how clever this fellow is. No, if I was plotting to murder someone, I would make sure this fellow wasn't around."

"When it came to murder or any crime," Uxtel said with a sad smile. "The Earthlings were quite inventive. Because of this, their law officers became quite inventive in solving crimes. I believe they had a whole science devoted to it."

"What? An entire science devoted to solving crime?" I asked. Perhaps a little too eagerly. "I knew other worlds had clever detectives, but having a whole science. That is scary and interesting. I have to meet this Earthling."

"Good luck with that, my dear." Queen Rexannis said with another smile. "I understand she moves him around a great deal, keeping him on a short leash. Don't misjudge Lady Venusun. She is quite fond of the

Earthling and does this for his safety. I would assume his actions have ruffled a few feathers, as the Earthling says."

"Still, I will meet him," I said, remembering that this ship was owned by Lady Venusun. After dropping off the happy couple, it was going to the lady's home world. I needed to change my travel plans. I knew the lady, but we weren't close. Still, I was a princess. I would play that card.

CHAPTER 14

AFTER DINNER

Sadly, the rest of the meal was devoted to discussing the Queen's wedding. Napkins folded into bird and flower arrangements were only of little interest to me. I quickly became bored and started to look around the dining room. There was the usual high society crowd, all with the same bored looks.

Oh please, we know you are rich.

What surprised me was that some commoners were in the dining room because of a lack of a better term. These interested me the most. How did they gain access to the executive dining room?

I made a note to speak with them. Commoners can be so interesting. They experience the world in different ways. I was raised in a bubble where my only contacts were other royal blood and servants who seemed entirely devoted to me. I now knew it was just their job, which confused me. Did they really like me?

Not important.

One very slender fellow, dressed in a brown suit that was either too big for him or just needed a good pressing, caught my attention. His face was relatively unremarkable. I would have overlooked him, but he kept glancing at our table. Everyone did, but this fellow seemed to be overly interested. If I didn't know better, I could swear he was looking for someone.

Perhaps an ex-servant, or even better, a soldier who had served under the Prime Centurion. That could explain his presence in the executive dining room. Still, I tried to figure out who he was looking at.

For this reason, my attention was drawn to the empty chair at the Captain's table. Someone had been invited but chose not to attend, and most anyone else would have been thrilled to sit among such people.

The word poker caught my ear.

"Yes, the Prime Centurion and I have invited the best poker players on board," Zana told the doctor. It should be fun."

"You haven't invited me," I said in an uninterested tone that drew the full attention of my fellow diners. Just what I wanted. I took a sip of water and smiled. "I have been overlooked. The Prime Centurion should remember me. Before the war, we played a few hands. I have a score to settle with him. Or did it slip his mind the last time we played he won the last round. Not interested in a rematch?"

The table suddenly became quiet.

I was confused. Had I committed some sort of social blunder? Was I not allowed to playfully mock the Prime Centurion?

"Oh, Princess Deela, forgive me. I was going to invite you right after dinner," the young Beta Chief said a little too quickly. I couldn't help but notice he glanced at the Prime Centurion, who looked confused. You will, of course, join us."

"How could I not after such a polite invitation," I said with a bow. "Just tell me when and where."

"My fiancé goes to bed early." Queen Rexannis said, glancing at her soon-to-be husband, who was still looking at me in a strange manner. It was like he was trying to remember my face. "As you most likely heard, he was injured during the war. Almost died. Because of this, he goes to bed quite early. The game will be tomorrow evening in the main parlor. I should warn you there will be some spectators. Apparently, some people enjoy watching others play cards. I do not."

"I love an audience, especially when I am winning," I said, noting the good Beta Chief's look as if he was about to protest. A mere glance from the Queen made him think better of it. Now that is settled, I will stroll around the decks."

CHAPTER 15

LONG ISLAND ICED TEA

I was wandering down the upper deck of the ship. Doors lined one side of the hall, but on the other were large windows that gave one an excellent view of the stars and planets. This has always fascinated me. The ship was traveling at a very high speed, but the universe outside looked as still as a painting, except for the occasional star or burst of light.

A star dying, perhaps?

It was during my stroll I came to an open door. I couldn't help but peek inside. It was a large room with dark wood paneling and a deep green rug. There were no windows and just this one door. There was a small bar made of dark wood with brass fittings. I stepped in and couldn't help but notice a table shaped like an octagon had been set up in the middle of the room with six chairs set up around it. There were no cards or chips, but this was the table where I would sit tomorrow night.

"May I help you, Miss?" asked the tall, skinny alien standing behind a short bar made of dark wood with brass rails along the bottom. His jacket and shirt were white. A red cummerbund surrounded the top of his black pants. The red bow tie around his neck looked too big because of his skinny neck. His yellow eyes and wide lips appeared eager to serve me.

"Yes, I think I would love an Earth drink," I said, walking up to the bar with a smile. "I don't suppose you could provide me with that?"

"As a matter of fact, Earth drinks have become popular. Especially the sweeter drinks. Ones with fruit and tiny umbrellas. I am happy to say I have become quite good at making them." He said, his wide mouth spreading into a grin that was a little frightening. "I can make you a cosmopolitan, mai tai, sangria, strawberry daiquiri, mojito, margarita, Pina colada, or a Long Island iced tea."

"What is a Long Island iced tea?" I asked, having heard of the others.

"A very deceptive beverage. It tastes like tea, but it has several liqueurs in it. Rum, tequila, gin..."

"You had me at rum. Please, my good fellow, make me one. I love tea."

"As you wish." He said, seemingly thrilled to be able to show off his talents as a bartender. "I must warn you. You can become intoxicated very quickly with this drink. I have seen men carried out after drinking just three."

"My good fellow, no need to tell me more. I am sold on this drink." I said as he quickly poured and mixed several things into a tall glass. He stirred them together, put a straw in the glass, and presented it to me with a flourish. I took a long sip and smiled. "This is delightful. Why are you down here in this small room? You should be in one of the upper parlors or the main bar. You obviously have talent."

"A thousand thank yous, miss." He said with a bow. "I usually work the main parlor on the top deck, but tonight, I was supposed to tend the bar here. There was supposed to be some kind of card game. But I have just been informed that it has been moved to tomorrow night."

"The game was supposed to be tonight," I said, sipping my delicious drink. I would definitely have another. "I am playing in that game. It is called poker. I was told it was tomorrow night. I wondered why they moved it. No matter. I found you."

"May I join, Your Majesty?"

CHAPTER 16

THE CAPTAIN'S TALE

I turned to find that the good Beta Chief Zana had entered the bar. He was now standing behind me, looking quite official in his uniform with its brass buttons and such. I know some females swoon at the sight of a man in uniform. I had never been impressed with military men. The ones I have encountered had no effect whatsoever. When I spoke to guards in my palace, I found myself talking to the top of their heads. Always bowing and so eager to please.

Not only dull but annoying.

Back to the Captain.

There was a smile on his face, but his eyes looked grim. Having been raised as a princess, good manners had been drummed into me. Most had been forgotten, but not all. I took another sip of my drink and smiled. "Please do; this very talented fellow has just introduced me to a drink called a Long Island iced tea. It is wonderful. Please have one. In the future, you may wish to remember when addressing a princess that it is Your Highness, not Your Majesty. That title is reserved for queens and kings."

"Thank you, your highness." He said with a bow. "That drink is a little too sweet for me. Can you make a Whiskey Sour?"

"Of course, Sir. I must tell you I do not have any Earth whiskey," the bartender said, looking slightly embarrassed. As you know, it is almost impossible to find. Pardon me, miss. Are you of royal blood? If so, I apologize for calling you miss."

"Yes, I am princess, but how do you know? It's not like we walk around in evening gowns with tiaras on our heads." I giggled. Perhaps the bartender was right about the effects of this drink. Better to pace myself. "How could I be offended? You just introduced me to this amazing drink. Now, what is a Whiskey Sour?"

"It is another Earth drink," Zana said with a smile. "But I don't think I ever had a real one. Apparently, a real Whiskey Sour requires whiskey from Earth. I heard Jack Daniels is the best."

"Captain, I am sorry to disagree, but while Jack Daniels is used, another Jim Beam is better known." The bartender said, not looking as apologetic as he should be. I suspect he was trying to impress me with his knowledge of Earth whiskey. I liked this fellow. "I understand whiskies called Colonel E.H. Taylor, Glenfiddich, and Telling are far superior. But I do have an excellent whiskey from Saldarous. Not Earth whiskey, but close enough."

"Well, I have learned something tonight. Let's give your whiskey a try."

I leaned forward to watch the bartender make the drink. "Are you putting an egg in there?"

"Just the egg white." The bartender said. "Gives it a nice foam on top."

I watched him shake a metal beaker and pour it into a small glass through a strainer. There was indeed foam on the drink. "That looks delicious. I will try that next."

"As you wish, Your Highness." The bartender said. "But there is an old Earth saying. Don't mix your drinks."

"Well, we will test that saying tonight."

"Your Highness, if I could have a word in private," the Optio said, glancing at the bartender.

After telling the bartender not to leave, I followed him over to the poker table. I settled down and gave Zana my best smile. "So, Optio, what is on your mind?"

"This is a delicate matter, but it needs to be addressed." He said, leaning forward. I did notice he had yet to taste his drink. "As you probably noticed, Prime Centurion Uxtel seemed confused by your mentioning you had a score to settle with him."

"Yes, I was somewhat put off. Uxtel was much friendlier in the past. Is this something to do with his injuries?

"The Prime Centurion was someone who led his men. He didn't sit back behind the lines. He was right in the middle of the battle. His men, including me, were so loyal to him. And as it turned out, he had the respect of the Earthlings."

"I would want my commander right there if people were shooting at me."

"Yes. During the battle of Talus, he is not only wounded but also captured. To our surprise, the Earthlings returned him to us. They did this because they were losing the battle and possibly wanted to curry favor with us."

"Clever. Did the Earthlings do the surgery on his face?" I asked. "I ask because it seems it's been done by an excellent hand."

"They saved his life, but the cosmetic surgery was done by us."

"Cosmetic surgery?"

"Sorry, I worked closely with some Earthlings after the war and picked up some of their jargon," Zana said too quickly as if he had made a social blunder. "Cosmetic surgery was their term for the procedures used on the General. My point is that his outer wounds could be cared for, but some wounds can't be fixed. The Prime Centurion suffered memory loss. He remembers some things, but much of his history is a blank."

"And the queen is still marrying him?" I said, sounding more abashed than I should have.

"They have known each other since childhood," Zana said with a frown. She still loves him and is convinced he will recover all his memories."

"A better woman than I," I said, wondering if I would make such a sacrifice. "Of course, I have never been in love."

"My point is the Prime Centurion may not be the player he once was."

"Ah! I see. If I am winning too many hands and the General is not, I shouldn't make much of it."

"Exactly, just play for fun. Who knows, you may help the Prime Centurion."

"I thank you for taking me into your confidence. I shall act accordingly."

"Thank you, your highness." He said, standing up, bowing, and quickly leaving without touching his drink. You can't just let a drink go untouched. I drank it in three gulps and ended up almost choking on it. This was no Long Island iced tea, but it was still enjoyable. It made me wonder how real Earth whiskey would taste. I went back to the bar and told the bartender to make me another drink. We decided on something called a Sangria. Once again, he gave me a ridiculous warning about mixing my drinks.

"Do you know why I am so good at playing poker?' I asked the bartender as he put together what promised to be another tasty drink.

"No, Your Highness. I don't know the game, but I know it is popular."

"Bluffing is a huge part of the game. I can tell when someone is bluffing. It's a gift."

"Bluffing, your Highness? I am not sure what you mean?"

"A big part of poker is trying to fool the other players into what cards you may or may not have. If you have a low hand, you try to bluff the other players."

"Are you saying you can tell when someone is lying to you about their cards, your highness?"

"Exactly."

CHAPTER 17

THE ENSIGN

Oh, by the blue moons of Dag, I wish I had taken the bartender's advice and not mixed my drinks. I, a princess, ended up bent over my toilet, throwing up. This is not to say I have not thrown up before, but never from drinking. Yes, I knew commoners suffered the downside of drinking too much, but I am of royal blood.

After this humiliating experience, I fell into bed fully clothed. The wrinkles and creases in my dress would never be ironed out. On top of this disaster, my head felt like someone was banging a drum inside of it. My whole body ached.

Fortunately, I remembered the bartender's advice about hangovers. He suggested eating a large breakfast and drinking coffee.

Since the man had been right about the effects of my drinking, he might be wise in curing these effects. I ordered a giant breakfast: eggs, fried potatoes, something called bacon, and sausages. The bartender recommended toast, and by incredible luck, the ship had actual Earth coffee.

I've had drinks similar to coffee from other worlds, but I've been told that Earth coffee is something special.

I must tell you that the meal was delicious and cured me of said hangover, but how had I survived this long without coffee? This drink was hot and so strong. Made even more incredible by adding sugar and milk. I had three large cups and felt like I had the energy to do anything.

After bathing and dressing in my best jeans and an Earth shirt called a hoodie, I assumed this was because it had a hood. It mattered not what it was called; it was comfortable. I put on a pair of Nikes and went to the parlor to find the young Ensign standing by the poker table. I glanced at the bar. No one was tending it. "Pardon me, do you know where the bartender is?"

"Good morning, Your Highness." The Ensign said dealing out cards to six empty chairs. "This bar doesn't open until tonight. If you wish to have a drink."

"Too early for that. I wanted to give the bartender who was here last night a tip."

"I think he is off duty, but he will be here tonight," she said, looking up from the cards and smiling.

"Excellent. You are playing tonight?"

"No, Your Highness. I am to be the dealer. It has been a while since I dealt with it, so I am getting in some practice. There can be no mistakes, considering who is playing."

"That would be me, the Prime Centurion, his loyal Optio, and the mysterious fourth player."

"There are to be five players. The ship's doctor will be playing. I don't know who the last player is. He keeps to his cabin. Never eats in the dining room."

"One wonders how he got invited to the game."

"He is a friend of the Prime Centurion. They served in the war together. Must be an odd fellow."

"Oh, he is not the only one," the Ensign said, smiling around. A passenger on the top deck stays in Lady Venusun's personal cabin. He or she came on board before the crew. Never leaves the cabin. Captain Fross has given strict orders not to disturb them."

"How does he eat? His food has to be delivered."

"The stewards are told to leave the food cart by his door. The Captain made clear anyone disturbing him or even attempting to catch a glimpse of him would lose their position."

"That is quite mysterious," I said. Then shrugged. "Probably a royal or some kind of famous singer or actor. They all have an exaggerated opinion of themselves. Fame and wealth will do that to you. But remember one thing, my dear Ensign."

"What is that?" she asked with huge eyes. Then, I noticed the points of her ears sticking out from under her hair. I would have thought she came from an entirely different world if not for the ears.

"Fate is a fickle bitch."

"What is a bitch?"

"Oh, it is an Earth word. It has several meanings but mostly refers to a mean-spirited woman. So fate is a bitch and fickle. She will turn on you with a snap of her fingers."

"That is a very frightening thought, your highness."

"Yes, it is."

CHAPTER 18

THE GAME IS ON

The rest of the day was relatively uneventful, except I saw the skinny fellow again. He was sneaking around on the top deck. I was about to confront him, but he must have seen me because he had quickly darted into the stairwell.

I was tempted to pursue the fellow, but I had more important things to do.

Such as deciding what I would wear for the game. Distraction is another part of the game of poker. One's attire could throw another player's game off. Since I was the only female at the game, I dressed accordingly.

I was wearing a very tight shirt called a tank top. It was bright pink with the word juicy printed across my more than ample bosom. I was not wearing a bra, so my nipples were there for all to see. Crude, I know, but so effective in distracting the males. My skirt was black leather with zippers on each side. Black and pink fishnet stockings and pink high-top sneakers completed my ensemble. I studied my reflection in a mirror and nodded my approval. The final touches were my pink framed sunglasses and a bright pink cap with the word pink printed on the front. I must admit I didn't understand why the word pink was on the cap. It was obviously pink.

A spray of perfume and a dash of lipstick. I was off. I made my way down to the parlor, walked into the room, and struck a pose. Hip tilted to one side. Hand on one hip. Chest thrust out. Smile on my face. Every eye turned to me. The room became silent. Several jaws dropped. Another great entrance. My smile brightened, and I said, "Let's play some poker."

I was making my way to the table. The onlookers parting to let me pass. I noted my favorite bartender looking over. I paused. "I think I will stick to wine tonight. Something red and sweet."

I came to the table. Still, all eyes were on me. The young Ensign stood there with a blush on her face. My pink eyes moved around the table. The Prime Centurion sat across from me in a white shirt and pants. Beside him, still in uniform, was the excellent friend Optio Zana. Still wearing his white dress uniform, Dr. Allton Crag sat by the Zana. Then came the Ensign and myself.

At last, the mysterious fifth player decided to join us. He wandered into the parlor without looking around, and the odd man slipped into the chair across from the dealer.

Suddenly, the cards flew across the table. The Ensign quickly apologized while gathering the cards, but her eyes were on the stranger.

I later found out his name was Daris. A common enough name which fit his common face. All in all, he was a most unassuming man, except for his skinny body. But closer examination revealed his suit was expensive and his fingernails polished and painted blue. It's not a custom in my world, but I understand it is quite fashionable in some. I studied him. He was the unknown factor in this game. How the man looked around made me wonder why he was sitting at this table. He obviously didn't want to be here.

On the other hand, with all his nervous tics and sweating, it could be how he played. Covering up all his tells with this act. I would have to be careful not to underestimate this fellow.

"The game tonight will be seven-card stud," Ensign said, sounding like she had regained control of herself.

"Excellent," I said but frowned when the Prime Centurion turned to a small table beside him. There was a wooden case sitting on it. He opened it, revealing a red velvet-lined interior. Inside lay a brown bottle with a long stem and two crystal glasses. He carefully lifted the bottle out. My curiosity piqued. I asked. "And that is?"

"Princess Deela, this is one of the finest Earth whiskies ever made. 1926 Macallan," Gar Way said, holding the bottle out so I could see the label. "Please don't ask for a sip. The bottle is half empty. I only take a drink on special occasions, this being my wedding voyage."

"I think sharing it with your soon-to-be wife would be more romantic," I said, thinking I really wanted to taste this whiskey or, even better, see what my favorite bartender could do with it.

"My fiancé has never acquired the taste for whiskey."

"Terrible stuff. I don't understand what all the fuss is about." Queen Rexannis said. I hadn't noticed the Queen standing in the corner, looking thoroughly bored, which is standard for all royals. I also noted the skinny man was standing in the back of the room. There wasn't much of a crowd. They were all here out of curiosity. I assumed they would drift away as the game proceeded. Poker is fun to play but not so much fun to watch; that's what I think.

"Are we ready to play, Princess Deela and gentlemen?" The Ensign asked.

I glanced down at the stacks of colorful poker chips in front of me. I won't bore you with the cost of buying into this game. It was high, but it wasn't an amount I couldn't afford; I expected to win. I picked up a gold chip and began to turn it over and over with my fingers. I saw the Prime Centurion looking right into my face. He was still handsome despite the scars. I gave him one of my best smiles and said. "Let the games begin."

"Eager to lose some money?" The Prime Centurion said, filling one of the small glasses almost to the rim. It had a very nice brown color, making me want a sample. As I studied the man across from me. I noted a trickle of sweat run down his face. The war had indeed changed Bacco Uxtel.

Such a shame.

The Prime Centurion toasted us with the glass and gulped it down. I swear his whole body seemed to shiver. He even let off a small gasp. He nodded to the Ensign, who began to deal as we all put a single gold chip into the pot. I leaned back, not looking at my cards. This was the time to study the faces as they peeked under their cards. The Prime Centurion showed nothing, but the Beta Chief raised an eyebrow. Since I hadn't played him before, I had yet to learn what this meant. Good cards? Bad Cards? The doctor actually grinned but quickly pressed his lips into a tight line. His eyes were bright. He had some good cards. The stranger showed nothing. This man might just be a player.

Excellent.

It's no fun to take money from bad players.

At this point, I lifted the edge of my cards and peeked.

Two aces.

I showed nothing until the Prime Centurion began to gasp for air. He struggled to his feet and grabbed his neck. His whole body violently shook, and then the man fell to the ground, still squirming and gasping. Then, he suddenly stopped moving.

For a few seconds, the room was filled with statues, and no one moved or said a word. Finally, I asked the question that needed to be asked: "Is he dead?"

CHAPTER 19

NOT SO FAST

"By the great god of dag, he is dead." I gasped as the doctor jumped and ran to the man's side. Queen Rexannis was just as fast. They both knelt around the body. The Queen begged her fiancé to wake up. The doctor undid the Prime Centurion shirt and began to feel around the man's face and body. He seemed to be making a big show of it.

I watched for a moment but then looked up. Optio was standing behind the doctor. The Ensign hadn't moved. Both had shocked looks on their faces. The man known as Daris just sat there sucking on his fingers. The man looked terrified. I looked around the room. My skinny friend was nowhere to be seen.

"I was afraid of this." Dr. Crag said, sitting back on his knees. "It is his heart. I gave the Prime Centurion a quick check-up after he boarded and warned him not to get too excited. I was against the game but agreed to play to keep an eye on my patient."

Well done, I was thinking to myself, but for some reason, I was not convinced the Prime Centurion had just died of a heart attack.

"My lord, we must move the body." The doctor said, looking quite grim. Queen Rexannis was slumped over the body, sobbing. Zana showed nothing. He just stood there like a good little soldier.

Captain Fross rushed into the parlor and took everything in. He nodded. "I want this room cleared right now. Everyone leave. The doctor and I will handle this."

"May I suggest you send for the queen's maids?" I asked. "Queen Rexannis seems quite distressed."

"An excellent suggestion, Your Highness." The Captain said. "Ensign Sig, if you could."

The young Ensign darted out of the room, looking thrilled to be able to leave the room.

I shall move ahead in the tale because it all became a muddled mess. Everyone, excluding myself, was escorted out of the room. I discreetly moved behind the bar and watched. Doing my best to avoid being noticed. Considering my attire, this was not easy. The maids, along with Prime Minister Tunga, were brought in. She took a long look down at the body, but there was something in her manner. I couldn't put my finger on it. The Queen was taken back to her room, leaving only myself, the Captain, the Optio, and the doctor. They were preparing to move the body when suddenly, a voice filled the room,

"Leave the body where it is. I have someone I wish to examine it."

Captain Fross looked up and around. Now very nervous. "Lady Venusun. I had no idea you were watching the game."

"Captain, I want a second opinion." Lady Venusun said in an icy voice. "Don't even think of protesting, doctor. We both know that your reputation is not without blemish. But what concerns me is how you became the Golden Halo's doctor. I didn't realize you were on board until I tuned into the game. But that is a matter for another time. For now, the body will be left where it is. Captain Fross, you will go get my employee from my suite. Tell him to bring his black case."

"Are you sure..."

"I have never been more assured of anything in my life. Princess Deela, stop hiding behind the bar. You may want to go along with the Captain. I assume you will want to meet the employee. He is an Earthling."

CHAPTER 20

THE EARTHLING APPEARS

I couldn't believe it. Not only was I going to meet an Earthling, but the one who solved murders and such. To say my heart was beating fast would be an understatement.

I eagerly followed the Captain up to Lady Venusun's suite. It was set apart from all the other cabins. There was even a security door that required a password. I hurried along beside Fross. He must have noted my eagerness because he slowed down and almost touched my elbow but caught himself.

"Princess, I know you wish to meet the Earthling," he said, looking grimly. I must warn you. I met several Earthlings, and this one is quite different."

"Oh, please. I have seen pictures and videos," I said, smiling when we approached the twin doors.

"Very well," He said and rapped on the door.

There was no answer, and there was another rap. I was still waiting for an answer. Finally, the Captain banged on the door and called, "Sir, I need you to come to the door. It is the Captain. Please. We both know I have a pass key."

I heard someone move close to the door. A muffled voice called out. "What do you want, captain?"

"Lady Venusun needs your assistance. It is very important."

I sucked in my breath as the door swung open. The Earthling appeared at the door.

To say I was disappointed is an understatement.

The Earthling was a little over five feet with a slender body that was a little wide around the waist, but he appeared to have no muscles. I could tell this because he wore a red striped bathrobe and slippers. His black, wiry hair was cut close to his head. Round, gold, wire-framed glasses rested on his nose. His brown eyes looked confused. But the most shocking thing was his skin was the color of chocolate.

"You are not an Earthling!" I gasped, the words coming out my mouth before I could stop them. And the words just kept coming. "But, you are all wrong. You are not tall enough. You don't have any muscles. Where are your tattoos? And you are the wrong color."

"Princess Deela, please!" The Captain gasped, giving me a horrified look.

The Earthling just looked at me with a slight grin. He reached up and tugged on his left ear. When the Earthling spoke, it was in a very soft tone, almost apologetic. His voice was quite pleasant, but he had a faint accent. He also seemed amused. "Ah, Princess Deela, you are not the first woman I have disappointed. You are just the latest in many. I can see you are a fan of the images on the different sites. But I assure you I am an Earthling. Considering how things are, why would I pretend to be one?"

"Your appearance is rather underwhelming," I said, trying to recover from my shock. "It just never occurred to me there were different kinds of Earthlings."

"Ah, well, Your Highness or, pardon me, is that the correct way to address you?" He said, looking a little embarrassed. "You are the first princess I have met."

"That or princess. Either one is fine. You were saying?"

"Oh yes, Earthlings come in all shapes and sizes. I will admit I am not the best example."

"Sir, we need your assistance in one of the parlors," Fross said, pushing his way into the conversation. I had many more questions, but there was a dead body in the parlor. My curiosity about this Earthling would have to wait. "If you could hurry along, Lady Venusun insisted and suggested you bring your black case."

"What is the problem, captain?" He asked.

"I suggest you come see for yourself."

I was about to tell, but a look from the Captain actually made me close my mouth.

Quite rude, but for now, I would hold my tongue.

"Oh, ah, well, let me get dressed," he said, looking distracted. Then he abruptly closed the door. It didn't take him long to change. A few minutes later, he wore a well-pressed black suit with thin lapels and an equally thin black tie. His shirt was white and appeared to be quite stiff. The cuffs of his shirt were folded back, and it had no buttons. Gold clasps seemed to hold them together. I noticed his well-polished black shoes.

"You have holes in your shoes?" I said.

"Ah, yes, princess. It's an Earth-style shoe called wingtips. Not my first choice, but my size is hard to find."

"I don't see any wings. Why would they call them wingtips?"

"Ah well, Your Highness, I didn't name them, so I have no idea why they are called wingtips." He said, giving another small smile before turning his attention to the Captain. "Shall we, captain?"

I looked at the square-shaped leather case the Earthling was carrying. It appeared to open at the top. The Earthling gave me a small smile and bowed and motioned for me to proceed. "After you, Your Highness."

Not a word was said as we trooped back down to the parlor. The Earthling seemed to be humming to himself. I didn't recognize the tune. An Earth song of some kind. I was familiar with the music. I enjoyed something called rock and roll and show tunes. Before I could ask, we were back in the parlor. The Earthling took two steps into the room and stopped. He studied the body and then said. "I would like to go back to my cabin now."

CHAPTER 21

THE EARTHLING'S FINDINGS

"Must you always be so droll?" Lady Venusun's voice filled the room but had an amused tone.

"Ah, Lady Venusun, this is the Prime Centurion Bacco Uxtel. I really think it would be best…"

"I think it would be best for you to do your job. The man is dead. The doctor says it was a heart attack. I don't have a high opinion of the doctor, so I want your opinion."

"You going to take the word of an Earthling over mine." Dr. Crag said, sounding aghast. He took a moment to glare at the Earthling. I was somewhat surprised. I mean, he was an Earthling. Everyone knows how they are. At least, I thought I did. Now, I wasn't sure. I will admit I was impressed with how he took the insult. I would not have, but I am a princess, and no one would speak to me in that manner.

"Lady Venusun," Optio Zana said, sounding equally shocked and angry. I could accept this. The Prime Centurion had been a close friend. "I can't allow this. This was a decorated war hero. A warrior of honor and courage. The idea of some Earthling even touching his body."

I noted the Earthling had moved closer to the door. Captain Fross stood with his hands behind his back. He glanced at the Earthling and shook his head. The Earthling let out a sigh that could be heard across the room. Everyone looked at him.

"Ah, ah, I assure you that I have no interest in getting involved with this for obvious reasons." The Earthling moved closer to the body and seemed to study it for a moment. "Ah, I was just wondering, was the Prime Centurion's skin tone always this pink?"

"No, proceed." Lady Venusun said with a colder tone but still seemed amused.

"Ah, if you insist, Lady Venusun." The Earthling said, kneeling down beside the body. He opened his case. Inside were small trays, like one of my jewelry boxes, pulled out in tiers. There were three rows of trays. The bottom of the case had other objects I didn't recognize, except the magnifying glass. He took out some blue plastic gloves and pulled them onto his hands.

"You are a detective!" I said with more admiration than I should have. Then I recalled the conversation about the Earthling who solved crimes.

"Yes, Your Highness, I was a detective back on Earth. I worked in homicide."

"Homicide? What is a homicide?"

"Murder, Princess Deela," Lady Venusun said from above. The Earthling specializes in murder. He has been helpful in other ways but shines in murder."

The Earthling ignored the comment and leaned over the Prime Centurion's face. He seemed to sniff. Then moved even closer to the dead man's face, almost touching it. After a few sniffs, he fell back on his knees and did the ear-pulling thing again. His gaze moved back to the poker table. He muttered something and went back to his case. From one of the trays, he took out a small round container. Inside were thin white strips. He took one out, went to the poker table, and studied the glass before putting the white strip inside. It instantly turned bright blue. Then he sniffed the glass. The Earthling seemed to like sniffing things. After this, he took the whiskey bottle and sniffed it again. He looked confused. Then looked at Captain Fross. "Captain Fross, could you get me a clean glass from the bar?"

"I'll get it," I said. I was moving before anyone could object. My favorite bartender was already holding out a glass. I took the glass back to the Earthling. He thanked me and poured a small dash of whiskey into the glass. Then, he obtained another white strip from his case. He dipped this into the whiskey, but this time, it stayed white. He studied the strip while pulling on his ear again. Then, he rubbed the side of his face and lips, sighing like someone about to deliver bad news. He looked up. "I am sorry, doctor, but I have to disagree with you. The Prime Centurion seems to have been poisoned. Mostly likely with some form of cyanide."

CHAPTER 22

THE GAME IS AFOOT

You can imagine the reaction of everyone in the room, even myself. An Earthling was accusing someone in this room of murder. Obviously not myself. I am above reproach. Still just coming out and saying it was the height of bad manners. I had always assumed everyone, even Earthlings, knew about social decorum. One does not blurt out someone has been murdered. The others were just as shocked as I was. They were soon pointing their fingers at the Earthling, even accusing him of the murder.

Which was utterly ludicrous. The Earthling wasn't even in the room. How could he have done it? Yes, I was shocked, too. That aside, the man was bolder than he looked. I suddenly wanted to know more about him.

A loud horn went off, and the lights flashed on and off. Then Lady Venusun's voice once again filled the room. "ENOUGH!"

This put a stop to all the finger-pointing and accusations.

"Explain." Lady Venusun asked in a very polite tone.

"Ah, ah, well, the color of the skin is pink. A sign of poisoning." The Earthling said, rubbing his hands together. "Then there was the smell of almonds on his breath. A good sign that it was cyanide poisoning. My test on the whiskey in the Prime Centurion's glass confirmed this. If there was no poison in the glass, the strip would have stayed white but turned blue. There is cyanide in that glass."

"But none in the bottle," I exclaimed. "The only poison is in the Prime Centurion's glass."

"Exactly, Your Highness." The Earthling said with a slight grin. "Unfortunately, this doesn't help tell us who poisoned the Prime Centurion. Since there is no poison in the bottle, it means someone put the cyanide into his glass."

"That is impossible." Zana snapped. "He took the glass out of the case, poured his drink, drank, and died."

"Ah, ah, did the general leave his case unattended at any time?"

"Yes." A small voice squeaked.

Everyone looked over at the ensign who had just stepped back into the room.

"While I was preparing the table," she said, sounding and looking guilty. When Prime Centurian came into the parlor, he placed the case on the small side table. He told me not to touch it."

"Did you?" Zana growled with the look of a hunter moving in for the kill.

"Of course not!" She gasped, looking shocked and offended. "I did not touch it. I had other things to do. The Prime Centurion left the case and joined you at the bar."

"Did you leave the case at any time?" the Earthling asked in an amiable tone, but he seemed to be studying her face. A smile came to his lips, followed by an ear tug.

"Yes, I tried to tell the general I had to go get fresh decks for the game. The players liked to see the unopened pack of cards. Then everyone watches while I carefully open it. I was only gone for a few minutes."

"But long enough for someone to open the case," the Earthling nodded. "Now, Lady Venusun, I suggest you put the body somewhere cold and seal off this room. I am sure the medical examiner will be able to tell you more."

"An autopsy!" Zana gasped, looking horrified at the prospect of Bacco's body being cut open. "This was a warrior of our world. A Prime Centurion. His body will not be touched. He will be taken home and placed upon a hero's pyre."

"Ah, is that the custom? I am unfamiliar with the customs of your world. So the body will be burned upon arrival?"

"Yes." Optio Zana said, snapping to attention with a smug, arrogant look.

"Not if I divert the Golden Halo to my home planet." Lady Venusun said in a calm voice. "A murder has been committed on my ship. I have my own reputation to consider. What will people say? A Prime Centurion murdered on the Golden Halo. I can hear the gossip now. Lady Venusun not only allowed someone to get away with murder but allowed evidence to be burned, making it impossible to find the said murderer. No, that won't do. Before you threaten me with Queen Rexannis, I have already spoken to Her Majesty. She agrees with me. The murderer must be found."

"Do you plan on letting this Earthling walk around the ship asking highly personal questions?" Crag said, sounding like this was just as bad as murder.

"He solves murders. This is a murder."

"Ah, Lady Venusun...this is not like the murder on Kalis." The Earthling said, looking nervous, not for the first time. "That was the butler murdering the maid to cover up their affair. This is...ah...involves a queen..."

"Oh, shush! I know you. You already have some ideas banging around in your head. You are like that little detective who talked about using the little gray cells. Well, my friend. The game is afoot."

"Ah, actually, Sherlock Holmes would have said that to his friend Dr. Watson."

"I knew that. I was just...oh, what is that Earth saying? Oh yes, I was pulling your chain." Lady Venusun said. "Captain Fross, you will inform the crew and passengers that they will all cooperate with the Earthling. Anyone who doesn't, you quickly inform me. If it is a crew member, tell them they will be terminated immediately if they hinder him. Optio Zana, I should tell you that if you interfere with the investigation, I will divert this ship to my home world. Am I clear?"

"You have made that quite clear." Beta Chief Zana said coldly, looking at the Earthling with disgust.

I, for one, had changed my opinion of this small Earthling in the nicely pressed suit. Suddenly, a fantastic idea popped into my head. "Oh please, Lady Venusun, could I possibly assist the Earthling. I have always wanted to write a book. I suspect this may be a great story to tell."

"I am not sure." She said, but I could almost tell she was smiling.

"Ah, ah, the princess might be helpful when talking to the Queen and other guests, considering she is a princess. She could take notes. I doubt she is involved in the murder. As far as I can tell, she has no motive to kill the Prime Centurion."

"The investigation, as always, is yours. But you are right. Princess Deela has no motive. Oh, princess, I love the outfit. You certainly have the figure for it."

CHAPTER 23

PRIME MINISTER LEY APPEARS

"A little too bright for my taste."

Annoyed, I spun around to find a tall woman with curly green hair and light green skin stepping into the parlor. She was lovely in a very garish fashion. The black and gold dress fell to her knees but was tight around her full figure. The V-neck was deep enough to give more than a hint of her well-endowed breasts.

I would have rolled my eyes, but since I have similarly displayed my bosom from time to time, who am I to judge?

On the other hand, she was a public figure who should have known more.

I noted her cheekbones were perfectly shaped, as were her nose and full lips. The powers that be had been very good to her, or perhaps a very gifted surgeon. I raised one of my eyebrows and coolly said. "Prime minister, it may be bright, but I wear it so well."

"You always do, Princess Deela," Prime Minister Tunga said with a tone that could almost be considered rude. I was tempted to remind her she was nothing more than an elected official and that I would be a princess forever. Still, she turned her attention to the Earthling. She studied him critically and said, "I have heard of you. I thought you would be taller."

"Ah, yes, my lack of height has already been pointed out to me by Princess Deela and many others. I have learned to live with it." He said, giving the newcomer a look over but seeming to avoid looking at those quite amazing breasts. Instead, his eyes drifted up until he looked her in the face. "So you must be Prime Minister Ley Tunga. I have also heard about you. Unlike me, you appear to live up to your reputation."

"I may not be of royal blood, but watch your tone, little man," she said with a hiss.

"Ah, ah, I meant no disrespect." He said, still in his neutral tone.

I do not like anyone who uses their position of power to threaten a person they consider beneath them. It is one of the reasons I left my world. I couldn't stand how my brothers and sisters ordered the servants. I mean, they are people, too. I stepped forward and said in my coolest voice, "He was not being rude or disrespectful. You, on the other hand..."

"Ah, ah, princess..." The Earthling said. "I really..."

"Princess Deela is right." Lady Venusun's voice filled the room. "You were being rude. Considering this Earthling has been given the authority to investigate this murder by myself and Queen Rexannis, perhaps I shall have a word with your queen."

"That won't be necessary, Lady Venusun," Tunga said, looking a little afraid. She stepped back and almost smiled. "You must understand. This is the first Earthling I have met face to face. I see now I was being overly sensitive. I do apologize."

Her apology seemed to be directed at Lady Venusun and not the Earthling. He didn't seem mad or annoyed but amused. It's like he was watching a scene in a movie being played out. Then, being ever so polite, he said. "That is all right, prime minister. No harm done."

Tunga almost said something but thought better of it. She simply smiled before looking down at the body. Her green eyes studied for a long while. For some reason, I wondered what was going through her head. Then she looked up at the Earthling. Another smile before she asked. "So you investigated murders before, Earthling?"

"Ah, ah, yes, I have. As Lady Venusun pointed out. Back on Earth, murder was my specialty." He said, looking right into her face. "Before Lady Venusun hired me, it had been a while, but it is kind of like riding a bike. You never forget."

Prime Minister Tunga was about to reply, but I quickly asked. "What is a bike, and what does it have to do with murder?"

Both the Earthling and prime minister looked at me. He just smiled. "It is an old Earth saying. It has nothing to do with murder. A bike is a two-wheeled thing that takes some time to learn to ride, but once you do, you never forget."

"Oh, I see. How clever." I said, now understanding. "You were saying you still know how to solve a murder. Quite good. I will have to remember that."

"Well, Earthling, I will leave you to your...murder," Tunga said, glancing down at the body. "Please let me know if I can be of any service to you. The Prime Centurion was an important man on my world."

"Yes, prime minister." I am sure we will talk again," he said.

The prime minister didn't even reply. She walked out of the room. I moved beside the Earthling and said. "I don't think she likes you."

"I'm not worried about that," he said, pulling on his ear. I'm curious why the Prime Minister was so mad.

"She wasn't mad."

"Yes, she was. She is a politician. They learned to mask their emotions, but I could see it in her eyes. I am unsure if she is mad because I am here or because the Prime Centurion is dead."

CHAPTER 24

GETTING TO KNOW THE EARTHLING

The Earthling asked Captain Fross to clear the room. Once this was done, he shut and locked the door. He returned to me and pulled out a small pad with a leather cover from his jacket pocket. A gold pen was attached to the binding. He held this out with a smile. "Ah, notes for your book."

"Oh yes, thank you," I said, taking the book and preparing to take notes. Still, I asked a question. "Do you smoke cigars?"

"No, princess, I don't." He said, going back to the poker table. He took a small round container and a small brush from his case. Inside the container was ink powder as bright as my hair. He began to carefully brush the powder on the Prime Centurion's case. Then, the bottle. Finally, the glass. "I once smoked a pipe, but my wife didn't like the smell."

"You have a wife?"

"Had a wife. She was on Earth...well, she was on Earth."

"Oh," I gasped, feeling bad for the small man. His wife had been on Earth when it had happened. I knew what we had done was wrong, but somehow, knowing the Earthling had a wife who had been killed made it more real. "I am sorry. I didn't mean to..."

"No need to apologize, your highness." He said, using another brush to sweep some of the powder away. Then he took out the magnifying glass and studied the pink marks on the bottle. While continuing to talk, he used clear tape to remove the marks from the bottle, glass, and case. "It wasn't your fault. My only regret was I wasn't there for her."

"Oh yes, that must have been very frightening for her," I said, watching him. "Are those fingerprints?"

"Yes, Your Highness. Ah, ah, I understand that it all happened so fast there wasn't time to be afraid. Still, one can't help but imagine things." He said without looking up. Then, he turned and held up two of the many fingerprints he had taken. "Perfect, don't you think? Before the war, we had a device that could copy fingerprints by scanning the surface. Fortunately, I took some classes."

"Yes, yes, very pretty," I said,

sad.

"Ah, remember to note that. It will add some color to your story."

I actually giggled at his small joke. Then he knelt by the body and carefully unbuttoned the Prime Centurion's shirt. We both looked at the hairless pink chest. The Earthling studied it for a moment, rubbing his chin. The magnifying glass was used to study the body's chest again. Then, he seemed to think briefly before using the magnifying glass again. This time, he examined the Prime Centurion's face and chin. More thinking and pulling on his ear. He took a small camera out of the case and took pictures of Bacco's face and neck. He checked to make sure the images were to his liking. "I could be wrong. Need to check."

"Check what?" I asked.

He quickly glanced at me, undid the Prime Centurion's sleeve cuff, and rolled it up. There were needle marks all up and down the arm. I gasped. "Bacco was a drug addict!"

"Ah, ah. No, I don't think so. The Prime Centurian was being injected with something, but I don't think it was a narcotic." He pointed at one of the marks with his gloved hand. "You see, he was injected with a very thin needle with two points. Addicts don't use that kind of needle. No, this was done for medical purposes. Hmmm, I have no idea what it could be."

You could look it up on the computer. I said, making some notes. Then I had an idea. "Can't we just take everyone's fingerprints and compare them? The murderer's prints might be on the glass or case."

"They may very well be, but I have my doubts," he said, taking another thin container from his bag with a printing card and small boxes on it. Inside the container was a black pad of what I suspected was ink. I watched as he pressed the Prime Centurion's fingers into the pad and then rolled them on the card, leaving an excellent print each time.

"That's brilliant," I said.

"Don't be too impressed. I am still an amateur when it comes to these old techniques."

"You seem to be doing very well."

"Ah, thank you, but everyone knew about fingerprinting back on Earth. The sad fact was they weren't really that reliable."

"Oh, someone told me you had a whole science for investigating crime."

"Yes, princess, it was called forensics. It was pretty amazing what those lab boys could do."

"So you did have a lot of crime back on Earth?"

"Yes, but as I am finding out, most planets out here do, too."

"Really? You think we are just as bad...oh my, sorry."

The Earthing was comparing the prints on the two cards. He lowered them and seemed to be thinking. It was like he hadn't heard me. Then he looked at me with a very calm face and said. "Twenty individuals got together and, in a matter of hours, decided the fate of my world. Oh yes, you have beings out here that are bad or worse than Earthlings. Ah, are you going to put that in your book?"

CHAPTER 25

REALITIES OF THE UNIVERSE

The Earthling did some more what looked like pottering around to me, except when he bent down and picked up the butt of a cigarette. He studied it before putting it into a clear plastic bag.

"A cigarette butt?" I asked. "There is a tray full of them over there."

"Ah, well, back on Earth, if I found a cigarette butt at a crime scene, I would get very excited. Very excited." He said, smiling as he talked. I was sure he was playing some joke. But then he said. "You can tell a lot from a cigarette butt. Take this one for instance. It is barely smoked. The smoker tossed it down and crushed it on this nice rug. Despite, as you have pointed out, Your Highness, there is an ashtray right over there. So they were enjoying a smoke, and something happened to make them crush out the cigarette with their shoe. We can assume they left in a hurry."

"Oh, probably when they saw the Prime Centurion die," I said, realizing that this Earthling was quite clever. "Anything else?"

"Yes, it was a woman, and they are rich."

"No, now you are playing me for a fool."

"No, no. You can see the lipstick on the tip. Interesting shade of green. You can also see the word Camel on the side of the butt. This is an Earth cigarette. Hard to find and very expensive."

"That's important. That would eliminate all the crew and most of the lower decks. The murderer is here on the upper deck. Someone of wealth and social standing did this?"

"It has been my experience that rich or poor, anyone can kill. You will notice I used the word kill. Most people can kill, but not everyone can murder. And yes, there is a difference, princess."

"I am not sure I would have liked your planet...on the other hand," I said, looking down at the body. "It appears we are more alike than I would have wished."

"Ah, ah...Princess Deela, do you really think my people would have gotten away with so much without help?" He started to pack his case. "Greed is a great motivator. There is no possible way the people of my world could have taken over so many planets without help."

"I...I..." I stammered.

The Earthling returned to the poker table, filled a clean glass with the whiskey, and returned it. He smiled and held it up. "Here, this might help."

CHAPTER 26

MY OWN PONDERINGS

I was sitting in the Earthling's suite. Actually, it was Lady Venusun's. It was much bigger than mine, with two bedrooms and a sitting room with a clear dome. This allowed me to look up at the stars and planets. It was richly furnished, but the furniture looked dated, or maybe it had been made to look that way. The walls were soft blue with light wood paneling, and the rug was another shade of blue, but I couldn't see any dirt on it. Was the Earthling cleaning for her, too?

Of course not; when he wasn't solving murders, he wasn't her cleaning man.

I was sitting in a round room with a long table with chairs. The chair at the head of the table had a very high back. The Venusun coat of arms was engraved into this chair. So, this was one of the many places Lady Venusun ran her vast empire.

Lady Venusun was royalty of some kind but didn't use the princess or queen. Everyone just called her Lady Venusun and never Milady. That included me. A princess. Sometimes, she called me by my first name, which was annoying, but I dared not object for some reason. I knew she didn't rule her world in a traditional sense. It was more like she ran it. To be honest, she ran numerous worlds. I had no idea how wealthy she was. I just knew everyone seemed to fear her.

Is fear the correct word?

She didn't use her power for any real goal that I was aware of. Obviously, she had amassed a great deal of wealth and power. It appeared she would only dabble in things from time to time. There was the story of a being on a planet she oversaw. There was a man who rigged the election to become president. He denied the allegations until the day he just vanished.

Mostly gossip.

But I have known people who she crushed because they betrayed her. I then realized I hadn't seen Lady Venusun publicly since the scandal with her ex-husband. Before this, she would have been seen at openings of all kinds, in clubs, and more. Now, she was virtually a recluse.

Was Lady Venusun nursing a broken heart?

"Deela, don't start thinking about these things," I told myself. "It is none of your business. Especially when it comes to Lady Venusun. Now, let's try to solve this murder. It would be fun to solve it faster than the Earthling."

I glanced at the closed doors. The Earthling had excused himself and locked himself inside the bedroom. It had been a good twenty minutes. I will admit I pressed my ear to the door but couldn't hear a thing.

Unsurprisingly, this was Lady Venusun's suite, with thick doors and walls. She was probably watching me and laughing, saying something like a silly princess.

"So what do we have?" I said to myself. "We have a dead body, poison, fingerprints, and a cigarette stub. Oh yes, the needle marks. Why did the Earthling take pictures of the face and neck?"

I slumped back. None of this made sense to me. "Very well, who wanted the Prime Centurion dead? Obviously, not the queen. Doubtful, the good Optio would want his old friend and commanding officer dead. There is the doctor. He would most likely have access to this cyanide. Was it hard to get? The impression I got from the Earthlings is that there is some form of cyanide on many planets. Some are more lethal than others. Oh, let's not forget the mysterious man who called himself Daris. He had vanished even before the Prime Centurion had been declared dead. Who was he, and did he want to kill Bacco? But the Prime Centurion invited him to the game. Deela, you fool. You have eliminated everyone except for the skinny man."

"What, skinny man?"

I almost jumped out of my seat. The Earthling had come back into the room without making a sound. How much of my musings had he heard? I blushed but regained my dignity and looked at the man with a smile. "I have been noticing a man wandering around on this level. Very skinny and wearing a brown suit. He obviously was a commoner. And he was in the parlor when the murder occurred."

"Mph, that is interesting. Point him out to me if you see him again. People being where they don't belong are more than likely up to some kind of mischief."

"I couldn't agree more," I said, standing up. So, what is our next step?"

"You may want to change, your highness." He said, looking me over but not in a nasty way, more clinical.

"Why?" I asked, putting my hands on my hips and, yes, thrusting out my bosom. He stepped back but didn't seem embarrassed. Did this Earthling have ice water in his veins?

"We're going to see Queen Rexannis. Your outfit is a perfect distraction when playing poker or attracting the...but...ah, ah. Maybe I am wrong. I am not a royal."

I looked down at my mostly pink outfit and realized it might not be appropriate. Rexannis was in mourning. "I think you are right. A change of clothes would be in order."

CHAPTER 27

THE GUARD

After I had changed into a simple black leather dress with matching cap and boots, I rejoined the Earthling, who showed no reaction to my new attire. I love to wear black. It's just so slimming. The Earthling's indifference to my appearance, beauty, and body was annoying. I was considered to be quite beautiful. The words exotic, wild, and yes, sexy were used. I had read that Earthling really enjoyed sex. They apparently had written books on it and even had different positions.

Different positions for sex.

Very intriguing. But this Earthling in his pressed black suit and white shirt. No, no, I couldn't see it.

I followed the Earthling down the hall to Queen Rexannis' suite. A large man in a black uniform stood in front of the door. His eyes looked over the Earthling. Then, with a deep, disapproving voice said. "Her Majesty is expecting you. She is a queen in mourning. Show respect...Earthling."

"Oh, sir, I wouldn't think of treating Queen Rexannis with anything but respect," the Earthling said in a very submissive voice. Ah, ah, are you stationed here all the time?"

"Only when the queen is inside. If she leaves, I follow at a discrete distance." He said, looking annoyed. I suspect he had been given orders to treat the Earthling with respect.

"The Prime Centurion didn't have a bodyguard?" The Earthling pressed.

"Obviously not." The guard said, looking right into the Earthling's face. "Or he wouldn't be dead."

"Ah, quite right. I was led to believe that before the war, Prime Centurion Uxtel did have a bodyguard?"

"Yes, before the war. The bodyguard, my brother, went with him to war. He was killed...by an Earthling."

"Those things happen in war."

The man seemed to be trying to intimidate while the Earthling passively stood there. The guard glared for what seemed ages. Then the Earthling said. "Ah, ah, the queen is waiting."

The guard's expression changed. Finally, he nodded and said, "The queen is waiting."

The queen was waiting for us in the sitting room. She was now dressed in black, with her hair pinned into a tight bun. A black veil covered her eyes, and she wore just a touch of makeup.

I thought this was odd.

She was supposedly in mourning. Two maids set up the small table for what looked like a snack. Once this was done, she motioned for the maids to leave. Once they were gone, she pushed up the veil, looked straight at the Earthling, and smiled. "Before you start to interrogate me. Allow me to ask one question."

"Ah, ah, I have no intention of interrogating you, your majesty." He said with a bow, but his face had a knowing look. "Your question."

"Was the person murdered tonight, Prime Centurion Bacco Uxtel?"

"No, he wasn't." The Earthling answered like he had expected her question.

CHAPTER 28

THE QUEEN'S SUSPICIONS

The queen's smile faded away. She slumped back and almost seemed ready to cry, but as queens must do, she did not.

I was ready to scream 'what,' but I had been trained like Queen Rexannis. Still, a gasp came out of my lips.

"Come, Earthling, we have much to discuss." Queen Rexannis said, sitting up and waving toward the silver pot and china cups. There were small triangle-shaped sandwiches. "I find myself in need of what you Earthling call a snack. Please join me. It is real Earth coffee. Princess Deela, would you please pour."

"Of course, Your Majesty," I said, taking a seat and pouring the coffee. It smelled wonderful. The Earthling pulled on his ear. Then, finally, sat down. He just kept studying the queen while she scrutinized him. Under normal circumstances, this would have been rude. These were not normal circumstances, and the queen wasn't objecting.

"The sandwiches are cucumber and cream cheese," Rexannis said, fluttering her fingers over the plate of sandwiches. "An Earth delicacy that I have become quite fond of."

"Ah, ah, I have never had one," the Earthling said, taking a sandwich and a small bite of one end of the triangle. He seemed to savor it and smiled. This is quite delicious."

"Yes, they are. Oh, cream and sugar in mine," the queen said to me, then looked at the Earthling. And you?"

"Black." He said.

I handed the Earthling his cup. I put cream and sugar into two cups and then gave one to the queen. She just smiled and took the cup. Then, like a true queen, she sipped and nodded her approval. The Earthling sipped his. I didn't sip. I gulped down a mouthful, sighing as that tremendous rush hit my body. Neither the Earthling nor Queen

Rexannis took notice. So I tried one of the sandwiches. Without thinking, I muttered. "Very tasty."

"Bacco enjoyed a cup of coffee with cream and sugar." Queen Rexannis said. "But when he returned, he started to take it black?"

"Is this when you began to suspect he was not your fiancé?" The Earthling asked.

"No, I had no suspicions at first. Bacco's changes, I assumed, came from the war and almost dying. Of course, the supposed memory loss. That will change anyone. Even the queen's consort."

"Ah, yes, your majesty. The memory loss. Bacco needed to relearn a great many things."

"This is true, but as time passed, I began to suspect his memory loss was selective. He remembered how to play cards and such, but when it came to his personal history. Nothing."

"Nothing?" The Earthling said before sipping his coffee. "Excellent coffee. But you accepted this at first?"

"Yes." She said, leaning forward. "Have you ever been in love?"

This made me look at the Earthling. If this question affected him, he showed no sign of it.

"Ah, hmm, yes." He said, taking a moment to adjust his glasses. "Deeply."

"Then you will understand. People who have been in love for a long time know each other. Bacco and I grew up together. We knew each other's heart and soul. Yes, we were lovers. The wearing of white was for tradition. I noticed little things. The coffee. His new fondness for Earth whiskey. But it was when we kissed that I knew. Now tell me how you knew?"

"Little things at first." The Earthling said. "The color of his skin. It was pink. On Earth, that is one of the signs of poisoning. Then, his chest was bare.

"All men in my world have bare chests."

"He was shaving his. I could feel and see the stubble on his chest. His beard was growing back. His red beard.

"There are no redheads in my world. Continue."

"Well, he had fingerprints."

"Fingerprints. Oh, the marks on one's hands. My people don't have those."

"Ah, I knew that, but the Prime Centurion did have fingerprints. The scars on his face and neck bothered me, so I took pictures and contacted a cosmetic surgeon I met during the war."

"What is a cosmetic surgeon?"

"Oh, that's a doctor who does face and body repairs and improvement," I blurted out. I believe Dr. Crag used to be one."

"A very good one, according to my friend." The Earthling said.

"It was very fortunate you could find him in such a short time, let alone contact him," Rexannis said, curiously looking at the Earthling.

"Thankfully, Lady Venusun is a very resourceful woman. Ah, ah, and there really aren't that many Earthlings left. Even fewer that are doctors of any kind." The Earthling said, this time showing just the slightest sigh of regret. "He confirmed whoever did the surgery on the man we now know isn't the Prime Centurion did a poor job. If I took him at his word, The Earthling said, Whoever did the work could have done a much better job. There would still be scars but not as....ah, ah."

"Severe?"

"Yes, Your Majesty. My friend said if he didn't know any better, he could have sworn the scars were made on purpose. I suspect Prime Centurion Bacco Uxtel was killed, and this person replaced him."

"Someone murdered my beloved Bacco?"

"Ah, ah, I can only say that, in all likelihood, he is dead. Why he tried to replace the Prime Centurion is still a mystery." He said, taking another bite of his sandwich. "This is quite good. Did the Prime Centurion leave the case containing the whiskey lying around?"

"Yes, and no, I didn't kill that man." Queen Rexannis said. "I will give you the man's death, which saves me considerable embarrassment. As you know, I was at the game. I wanted to watch this man play. Princess Deela will tell you how each person plays poker has his own style."

"Oh yes, tells, bluffing," I said. "We all do it but not in the same way."

"I have played poker." He said with a smile.

"I suspect you were very good at it," the queen said, taking a sandwich and nibbling it.

"Ah, well, I used to play with the boys back on Earth," The Earthling said, looking as if he remembered a happier time. "They stopped playing with me."

"Why?" I asked, thinking this was quite rude.

"I kept winning."

"I imagine you did," Rexannis said, finishing her sandwich. "So, who is this man?"

"I have no idea. Ah, ah, if I had my way, I would have the body be put in an airlock and dumped into space."

"Why?" I gasped, looking at the Earthling.

"He suspects the man may be an Earthling." Queen Rexannis said with a grin, then sipped her coffee.

CHAPTER 29

THE EARTHLING'S THEORY

I looked at the Earthling, who did little more than shrug and turned his attention back to Queen Rexannis. "It is more than a fear. It is a logical conclusion. The only people who would benefit from this plot would be Earthlings. It also explains why the Earthlings returned him after his capture. I worked in what you might call Intelligence during the war. I was involved in similar plots but not on this scale. I knew the name Bacco Uxtel. Am I wrong to think his pro-Earthling feelings came after the war?"

"No." Queen Rexannis said with such firmness it made us both look up. "Before the war started, he met several military officers from Earth. He grew to...not like but respect their attitude regarding honor and service. Then the war came, and he did his duty. More than once, he remarked to me with a smile, 'These Earthlings know how to make war.'"

"I couldn't disagree with him on that." The Earthling said with a shake of his head. "Centuries of practice do make one an expert. But I understand you didn't see the Prime Centurion until after the conference on Earth's moon."

"No. So you think the switch was made before the war ended?" Rexannis said, now interested.

"I can't tell you when or where the Prime Centurion was replaced." The Earthling said, pouring himself another cup of coffee. He held the pot out. The Queen and I declined. "Now, as I understand it, the last battle Prime Centurion Uxtel was in was very close to Earth. It was there his ship was captured, along with him. As I said, I don't know if your fiancé was killed or murdered. I do suspect this was when the switch was made. I think it was a desperate ploy to save our world."

"How?' I asked, wondering how one man could save an entire planet.

"Ah, ah, working in Intelligence, I began to hear rumors of the final act. Toward the end of the wars everything was happening so fast. The Unification of Planets was close to keeping their word by finishing the war and making the Earth pay. Many planets, including yours, wanted revenge. I understand that. What was not known was there was a revolt on Earth. The people who started the war. Corporate leaders, politicians, even the president found themselves up against the wall."

"Why would they put these people against a wall?" I asked, really not understanding.

"Princess," Queen Rexannis interrupted with a smile. "They were shot."

"Oh!" Suddenly, I felt foolish.

"Please continue, I find this fascinating."

"The Earth was in turmoil. The war was ending. Our planet was surrounded by Unification ships. The new leaders of my world sent out a delegation for peace. That's where I was when I learned the actual plans for the final act. The decision on how to go forward was still being debated.

"General Bacco Uxtel was one of the loudest voices against it." The Queen said. "No, not my beloved, but an Earthling posing as him."

"By the God of Dag, that is horrible." I gasped, looking at the Earthling, who smiled sadly.

"The delegation was arrested and told they would be put on trial." He continued. "By this time, my group had been captured and held on one of our own moon bases. We were to be tried, too."

"There were no trials?" I said. "Every Earthling was let go after the war."

"My dear princess," Queen Rexannis said with a sad smile. "It is one thing to talk about destroying an entire world. It is another to actually do it."

"Exactly." The Earthling said. "They went ahead with the final act. Many centuries ago, the Earthling who helped create the first nuclear weapon was supposed to have said, 'I am death. I have become the destroyer of worlds.' I assume he instantly regretted what he had created."

"According to the man posing as Bacco," The queen said. "Seconds after the destruction of your world, those twenty people realized they had gone too far. Did you know four committed suicide within months? No one involved was unaffected."

"Yes, Lady Venusun told me." He said, putting down his cup and sitting back. "The remaining Earthlings were given pardons and released."

"Now I understand," I said with a faded smile. "The imposter was supposed to stop the final act. He failed, but why did he continue the façade? He couldn't expect to fool the queen. There was the wedding night."

"They needed to keep the Prime Centurion alive so he could continue to fight for the rights of Earthlings. Bacco Uxtel was respected, rich, and powerful. Only one thing stood in the way of his plan's success.

Queen Rexannis looked right at the Earthling and said. "Me."

CHAPTER 30

COMPLICATIONS

"Yes," The Earthling said as cool as you please. "Ah, I think this imposter planned to murder you before you reached your home planet. Then he would be free to continue on as the Prime Centurion."

"That's ridiculous," I said with a shake of my head. "Someone would have guessed."

"Probably not for a long time. Ah, I suspect some people in your home world wouldn't care." He said, looking at the queen. "Ah, ah, I am guessing your death would throw the politics of your world into turmoil."

"Yes, it would," Rexannis said, looking right back with that knowing smile. I suspect you already know. Thanks to the war and a questionable plane crash, I am the last living member of the royal family. If I die, the royal bloodline dies with me. To some people, that wouldn't be a bad thing."

"Ah well, I know your world has a parliament and prime minister, but the real power still rests with you."

"Much to Prime Minister Tunga's dismay. She has made no secret of the fact that, in her mind, the royal family has outlived its usefulness. Happily, I am still loved by my people, and she is not so much. She does try. Tunga is quite pretty and has a full rich body that she has no problem using to distract...well, let's say her face and body is an advantage."

"She does that. You should have seen her ads when she was campaigning. Luckily, royals don't have to deal with such foolishness." I said. Suddenly, I recalled my sister's wedding. It had taken almost a year to plan. "A royal wedding takes time to plan, but this has all been done in less than a month. Your majesty, you wanted to get married as quickly as possible."

"Ah, yes, her majesty wanted to..." The Earthling said.

"Create an heir for the throne as quickly as possible." Queen Rexannis said. "Those plans are now dashed. It will be at least another year before I consider getting married. A time of mourning is expected."

"Ah, yes, but the death of Bacco puts your life in more jeopardy."

"I agree," the queen said. That is why I have no intention of leaving my suite until we reach Sirona."

"Sirona?" I asked. "The ship is changing course?"

"Yes, Lady Venusun and I agreed that it would be safer for me not to return home at this time." The Queen said, "I am hoping you will solve this problem before we arrive there."

"Ah, hmp, your majesty, I am just trying to find out who killed the fake Prime Centurion. I don't want to get involved with the politics of your world."

"Oh please, I can see you are no fool. You must know this murder is about the politics of my world. You find the murderer, and you find my enemies. Here is a thought. Perhaps the imposter had planned to poison me. Sharing a glass of whiskey at a romantic moment."

"And he got the glasses mixed up." He said with a shake of his head. "Ah, no, no. The Prime Centurion was the target. Your political enemies back in your world would never try to kill you. The public outrage."

"I agree. My opponents will now have to at least try to wrestle power from me, pointing out I am the last royal. I consider that an advantage. You are right; the imposter was the target. I need to know who was behind this plot. I need to know what happened to my Bacco."

"Ah yes, he could have been killed because he was an imposter."

"I suggest you find the murderer then," Rexannis said, tilting her head. "Even though I am not a detective, I suggest you talk to Prime Minister Tunga."

"Ah, ah, thank you for the advice, but I think talking to Beta Chief Zana would be more interesting. He was with the Prime Centurion."

"Do keep me informed," she said. One of the maids then appeared, signaling that the interview was over.

"Thank you, your majesty." The Earthling said, standing up and then picking up three triangle-shaped sandwiches. Then he smiled. "Ah, ah, something to munch on while I investigate. I think it is going to be a long night."

"It already has been," Rexannis said, picking up a sandwich and biting into it.

CHAPTER 31

WHAT THE GOOD OPTION KNEW

The Earthling and I were escorted from the queen's suite. The guard glanced as we passed. The Earthling took my elbow but quickly dropped his and motioned me to follow him down the hallway. Under other circumstances, I would remind him of his place. I had decided we were partners in this investigation and let it pass. He led me to the end of the hallway and looked around. He moved in closer and whispered. "Ah, princess, I think it is best we keep the fact that the Prime Centurion might have been an Earthling to ourselves."

"But why? We know he was an imposter." I said.

"Ah, mph, yes we do." He said and thought for a second. "What we don't know for sure is if he was an Earthling. We won't know for sure until the autopsy, which is one of the reasons we are going to Lady Venusun's planet. There will be no one to protest the autopsy."

"Yes, I can see that. Considering you are an Earthling, some people would object. They might even blame you for this whole thing."

"Ah, exactly, and what we don't have is a clear motive. Was the Prime Centurian killed because he was an imposter or because of the coming wedding? Either way, finding the murderer would only create more problems. If it turns out to be Prime Minister Tunga or another Earthling, the fallout would be dangerous for me and you. You understand?"

"Yes, you're right," I said, and another idea popped into my head. Right out of the blue. A brilliant thought. "Wait, there has to have been another imposter on board. Whoever he was couldn't have expected to pull this off by himself. The question is, who? Wait, you have someone in mind."

"Optio Zana was on the same ship as the Prime Centurion."

"Oh, oh, he was captured too and has scars!"

"Now you see why we must be careful. Although not from the right social class, Optio Zana was still the Prime Centurion's right hand."

"Yes, this is getting very complicated and dangerous for you," I said, remembering he was an Earthling, which was odd. When did I forget that? "So, are we going to see the Optio?"

"Yes, ah, ah, be careful, princess." He said with a small smile. If he is involved, the Beta Chief will try to get information from us. Ah, ah, ah, I have noticed you tend to blurt out your ideas."

"I do not!" I said, feeling offended and, well, embarrassed. I could feel my face blush. The Earthling just stood there, showing nothing. My anger left as quickly as it had come. The fact was my mother, father, sisters, brothers, and friends had pointed this out to me more than once. Putting on a brave face, I simply said. "I will let you do all the talking."

"Ah, that is very kind of you, Your Highness, but if something does occur to you, feel free to share it."

"Of course, we are in this together."

The Earthling actually laughed. "Are we?"

Optio Zana's suite was smaller than mine, which didn't surprise me. Just two rooms and a bathroom, all decorated with nautical décor. The floor was free of any clutter except for the captain's jacket and tie. Both had been taken off and thrown to the floor. There was a bottle of some kind of liqueur I didn't recognize. He had apparently kicked off his shoes after sitting down. There was a large tumbler filled with a brown liquid in one hand. He did not rise when we came into the room.

He didn't even answer the door. He just yelled that it was open. Apparently, the death of the Prime Centurion had made the good Optio forget his manners.

I was about to comment on his rudeness; it is common knowledge that one should always rise when anyone of royal blood enters the room, but the Beta Chief spoke first.

"I don't like Earthlings," Zana said, eyeing the Earthling. His voice was hard and bitter, as well as it should be. "I didn't share the Prime Centurion's generous feeling toward them. Your kind caused too much death and destruction. I lost family and friends."

"Ah, ah, well, sir, you are not alone in those feelings." The Earthling said, studying the officer with a small smile. He took off his glasses and began to polish them with his handkerchief. "It has been a long night for everyone. I would prefer to be in bed, but here we are. So we must make the best of it. No games. I think we owe each other that. I won't ask you the usual questions. Because, well, ah, I know the answers. So, let's start with the obvious one. You were captured along with the Prime Centurion?"

"Yes, you are right. We do owe each other the truth." Zana said, sitting up and looking at the Earthling. "I can tell you know more than you should. I had heard of you and how clever you are. I was pleased that you have found something most of us could not. The Prime Centurion and I were caught together but not held in the same place. He was Prime Centurion."

"Ah, yes, he was," the Earthling said, holding up his glasses and checking to make sure they were clean before putting them on. That's better. I can now see you much clearer. Should I bother to ask if you noticed any differences in Prime Centurion Uxtel after his release?"

"No. No games. As they say back on Earth. This was all big-picture stuff. Desperate times call for desperate measures."

"Desperate enough to kill a queen?"

"Yes." He said, suddenly looking right up at the Earthling.

"Ah, no disrespect, but it was a terrible plan."

"It was never supposed to go this far. The original plan was just to stop the final act. Bacco saves the Earth and then dies in some manner. Life goes on. We failed."

I will admit I am not the most intelligent person I know, but it was then that I realized the good Optio was an Earthling. I stared at his face and asked, "You are an Earthling?"

"Yes," Zana said, lifting the glass and gulping his drink. He smiled at the Earthling. "Jack Daniels. I am down to my last few drops."

"Ah, sir, I need to know..."

Zana began to gasp. He looked at the glass in his hand and then at the Earthling. The man staggered to his feet and stumbled toward us, reaching out but then collapsing to the floor. I jumped back, squealing, afraid he had something catching.

The Earthling rushed forward and knelt down by the captain. He turned the man over and looked into his face, but it was too late.

"He's dead?" I asked

"Yes," the Earthling said, laying the captain's head down. He stared at the face for what seemed ages. I have to contact Lady Venusun. Poison. The Beta Chief has been murdered."

CHAPTER 32

A THIRD EARTHLING

Once again, the Earthling went through the same motions as before, but this time, the poison was in the whiskey bottle, not the glass. Fingerprints revealed that the good Beta Chief was not who everyone thought he was. Once again, the poison called cyanide was suspected and then confirmed by the little white strips.

The other difference was the Earthling insisted the ship's doctor not be brought in. Captain Fross objected until a call was made to Lady Venusun. I was there, so I can clearly state that Lady Venusun had complete faith in the Earthling and made it clear he was in charge of the investigation. My name came up, too. She implied that I was working with the Earthling to solve these murders.

Always nice to be appreciated.

Once this was made clear, the Earthling didn't give orders like I would have, instead strongly suggesting that this second murder be kept secret. No one was to know. Fross was uncomfortable with this, pointing out there were more than a few important beings on board. The Earthling was more consenting than I would have ever been. He told Fross he would inform the queen himself, which seemed to make the captain much more agreeable, then made it clear that Prime Minister Tunga was not to be told.

That all done, he turned his attention to the cabin and me.

"Ah, ah, well, Your Highness, do you have any thoughts?" he said, wandering around the room. He picked up the bottle of what I now knew to be Jack Daniels whiskey and muttered what a shame it was to ruin good whiskey.

I couldn't have agreed more. I would have loved to taste it. "Could the captain have killed himself? I mean, we both now know he was an Earthling. With all due respect, he would be facing severe punishment."

"Ah no, the look on his face was completely surprised." The Earthling said, going into the bedroom. I followed and was surprised at the mess. The bed is unmade. There were clothes on the unmade bed and lying on the floor. There were even dirty dishes on the side table and floor. I was appalled and said so. He turned back and smiled. "Yes, it is quite a mess, back to Optio. He reached out to us for help. I suspect his hope was that the queen would try to cover up the fact that an Earthling had fooled her. Perhaps let him go."

"Impossible," I said. "Queen Rexannis would never let him go. She would want to know the true fate of Bacco Uxtel. The Beta Chief was the only one who knew."

"He would have used that to bargain with her." He said, moving around the room and avoiding the mess like I was. The Earthling seemed as disgusted by the mess as I. He would pick something up only with his gloved hands, then drop it, rubbing his fingertips as if trying to get the filth off. "I suspect the Optio was counting on Queen Rexannis wanting to know how her fiancé died. Still, whoever this man was, I doubt he was a military officer. The state of this room. Even after the service, most officers maintain the same need for order. Ah, oh, princess, Optio is not the only one who knows the fate of the Prime Centurion. This conspiracy was not dreamed up by just two men. No, this is a bigger plot than that."

"My word!" I gasped and looked around the room like I was looking for someone. "Are you saying there might be another Earthling on board?"

"I don't know for sure, but I wouldn't be surprised," he said and drifted away momentarily.

"Are you all right?" I asked, now concerned.

"Fools. This entire plot confirms all the bad things other worlds think about Earthlings. We were making progress, but this could be used to undo everything. People would start hunting Earthlings again. I need to think."

"About who the murderer is?"

"No, I have to decide if I really want to solve this. It might be best just to let the murderer get away."

CHAPTER 33

JUST A COP

"WHAT!" I screamed and walked up to the Earthling, putting my hands on my hips and looking him in the face. "You must find this murderer. You can't just let him kill two people...two Earthlings. Two of your own kind."

"Ah, ah, you are right." He said, looking at me with sad eyes but a smile on his lips. "As we used to say back on Earth, 'I am a cop. It is a dirty job, but someone has to do it.'"

"Cop? Are you a cop? I thought you were a detective?"

"It's another name given to law officers back on Earth. Centuries ago, law officers wore badges made of copper. I guess the bad guys started to call them cops for short. It was considered an insult but a word we used among ourselves."

"So you would call each other cops, but if someone else called you a cop, it was considered an insult?"

"Yes. I may work for Lady Venusun, and I suspect some of her business ventures are less than legal, but I am still at heart a cop. I suspect there is another Earthling on board. It will be difficult to find him. The Prime Centurion and Beta Chief were open for everyone to see. Mere pawns being told what to do. This last one will be doing everything in their power to go unnoticed. I suspect he is the ring leader."

"Ring leader? Another Earth phrase? Your language is very confusing. Not very precise."

"Ah, ah, yes. It appears we Earthlings used more slang terms than most other planets. I mean, this last Earthling is the one in charge. Now, let's find the doctor. I don't think he will be in his cabin. I suspect he will get drunk in one of the smaller bars on the ship. It is my understanding he has a history of drinking."

"Yes, I have heard that, too," I said, ignoring that several people have pointed out that sometimes I may drink just a bit too much.

"There is no place for him to run. We are on a ship in space. He will be waiting for us. At least that's what I would be doing."

CHAPTER 34

It took us quite a while to find the doctor. He was in a bar on the lowest level in the ship's rear end. I swear I could hear the engine vibrating through the walls. The bar was tiny, with three tables and a very short bar made of scratched, unidentifiable wood. It also looked like someone had been putting cigarettes out on it. The place was dimly lit and had a very cheap feel to it. The fishnets and plastic sea life used for decoration didn't help.

The bartender was overweight, with orange skin with purple dots. His uniform was wrinkled and stained with something disgusting. He probably hadn't bathed in a while, and a closer study made me think he might be intoxicated, too. It's not a very good place to drink.

The Earthling took it all in and smiled as if he approved it. I moved beside him and asked, " Do you like this place?"

"It reminds me of Earth." He said, wandering around and touching a plastic fish in the nets. He wasn't wearing his gloves, making me even more disgusted. "Back on Earth, when I was a cop, I lost count of the cheap bars I visited. Criminals like places like this. I must ask Lady Venusun why she decorated a bar this way. It would be interesting to know her reasoning. Ah, there is the doctor."

Dr. Crag was sitting more slumped over a table in the corner of the bar. The place was so dark I almost missed him. He was dressed casually: a loose shirt with a loud flower print, red shorts, and open-toed sandals. It appeared he had not shaved or combed his hair recently. On closer examination, I saw the shirt was stained with yellow. I kept my distance. There was a large bottle of Yung-to gin in front of him.

No one drinks Yung-to gin.

Well, someone must. They make it. Well, what I mean is no one I knew drank the terrible stuff. I just assumed it was awful because I had been told so and had never seen it before, except in ads for the media channels. The clear bottle was half empty. He was raising a glass to his lips when he saw us. The doctor smiled, toasted us, and gulped it down. "I have been expecting you."

The Earthling glanced at the bartender and smiled. "Ah, ah, it might be best if you take a break?"

At first, he looked at the Earthling with surprise and was about to respond. I jumped in. "You heard him. Take a break, or shall I call the captain?"

The bartender quickly left.

"Ah, thank you, princess." The Earthling said, walking up to the table and watching the doctor pour another drink. "You are out of uniform, doctor."

"Oh please, Earthling, you know Lady Venusun informed me that my services will no longer be needed," Crag said, looking into his drink and smiling. "My services will no longer be needed. Ha, ha. There was a time when my services were very much in demand. Kings, queens, presidents, and more came to me. To me, Earthling."

He gulped down the drink and slammed the glass down on the table. The doctor lifted his hands and stared at them. "These hands could work miracles. I made the ugly beautiful. Then one tiny mistake."

"Hardly tiny, doctor," I said, annoyed with his rude, drunken behavior and arrogance. "You disfigured a princess."

"I could have fixed it." He snarled up at me. "Another supposed colleague corrected it. Did you know that?"

"Yes, it was corrected by a surgeon who wasn't drunk." I snapped back, knowing the whole story very well. I didn't get it firsthand, but I did hear it from my sister, who heard about it from her best friend, who heard it from someone else she completely trusted. "Looking at you now, I can see the story is true."

"I was not drunk...two glasses of wine..."

"Ah, hmp, ah. Please, we are getting off track here." The Earthling said. "I didn't know Lady Venusun had let you go. She only tells me what she wishes. And being honest, I don't know or care how you lost your reputation. I now believe you are gifted. Only a gifted surgeon could have done what you did. Make an Earthling look so much like someone from Icakka. Fooling so many people. Impressive."

"Yes, it was. The scars weren't necessary. I told them the scars would only draw attention to the face, but they insisted. There have to be scars. If they had listened to me, that fool would be Prime Centurion Bacco Uxtel's twin. It would have worked; it fooled the queen. Fooled everyone. Now, my greatest work will land me in prison. I suppose telling you I was forced would not help."

"Doctor, I am an Earthling. I have no idea what will help you." The Earthling said, sitting across from the doctor and picking up the bottle. He studied the label, then sniffed it. "I would think you picked a better gin. These could be your last drinks for a long time. Ah, ah, I have my doubts about you being forced. I suspect it was more of an act of desperation. I saw your military record. There is no record of you being captured, but the military hospital you worked at was captured."

"I was doing good work there," Crag said, taking the bottle and pouring himself another drink. I not only saved a lot of lives but also gave them back their faces, hands, and legs. Those men and women went home to live everyday lives. Thanks to me."

"The war was ending. Yet the Earthlings seemed to intend to capture that hospital...they wanted you."

"Yes, they came for me," Crag said, looking up at the ceiling and smiling.

"Just like kings and queens." The Earthling said, leaning forward. "They offered you your old life back in exchange for doing some surgeries for them."

"Yes, yes. Well, not completely." The doctor said with wide eyes. He gulped down his drink. "I could never get back the life I had, but something close to it. All I had to do was help them save the Earth. After this was done, the imposters would get their old faces and bodies back. Then, I would practice on your own Earth. My patients would be only the rich and powerful."

"But they didn't save the Earth," I said, still standing. "You somehow ended up here."

"By then, I was the Prime Centurion's personal physician," Crag said, turning his attention to the Earthling. "I was there when they destroyed your world. It is something I will never forget. All but two leaders were horrified. All of them were sick to death. Everyone shocked. Some were vomiting. Two were on their knees, begging their gods to forgive them. One who was unaffected left in disgust, calling them weak and fools. Odd, he was the first to die. Shot himself."

"Ah, ah, when did they decide to keep up the charade?" The Earthling asked, keeping a calm look, but his eyes revealed the doctor's comments had touched him.

"Almost immediately. The Earthling in charge, I don't think he was in the military. He felt more like a politician. You Earthlings would call it slimy or nasty.

"This Earthling. Is he on the ship?"

"There are three Earthlings on the ship. The Prime Centurion was one. Optio Zana is another, but I suspect you have figured that out. The last one was on board until the game. I was as surprised as anyone. But there he was. His new face and body. He was my masterpiece. Odd because I hadn't seen him since the moon base. He just turned up here. What is that Earth saying? Is it something to do with a bad penny?"

"The last player?" I asked. "The stranger who looked like he didn't want to be there?"

"What stranger?" The Earthling asked, looking at me.

I was about to answer when a loud boom filled my ears, making them ring. The next thing I knew, the Earthling pushed me to the floor.

How rude.

I screamed for him to get off of me but then saw the doctor's face, or what was once his face. The large bloody hole had replaced a great deal of it. I have obviously never seen anything like this. This appalling sight made me scream even louder. Worse, I felt my evening meal rushing up my throat. I managed to avoid this humiliating scene. Then I realized the Earthling was no longer on top of me.

CHAPTER 35

THE PLOT THICKENS

"Ah, ah, you are telling me there are no cameras on this ship?" The Earthling was asking Captain Floss. As for myself, I kept staring down at the large weapon lying just outside of the small bar. Smoke was still drifting out of the barrel of the awful thing. This greyish stream of smoke was rising into the air, filling the hallway with a nasty smell. Apparently, someone had fired this thing and killed the doctor. The shot had been so loud it had brought a steward and some passengers into the hallway. If the killer was among them, I couldn't tell. Then I noticed the Earthling was still standing by the dead doctor. "Don't you want to see this thing?"

"Ah, hmp, your highness, if I move any closer to the pistol, I could be arrested."

"Really? Why?" I asked and then realized the foolishness of my question.

Captain Fross, along with Ensign Sig, had joined us. He had attempted to get a better look at the dead body, but the Earthling stopped him. Something about contaminating the scene. This time, Fross didn't object. More crew members arrived, and they made sure the hallway was clear. While this happened, the Earthling asked the captain to see the footage from the camera in the hallway.

I need clarification.

Why would there be cameras in the hallway? Using cameras to spy on the passengers?

More than a little rude. Downright impolite.

"Of course, there are cameras!" Fross snapped, looking quite offended, even putting his hands on his wide hips. "There are cameras on the crew's deck, engineering, and, of course, in the casinos and the smaller gaming rooms. But there are no cameras in the hallways or in the rooms. This is the Golden Halo."

The captain said this as if this was as good an explanation as needed.

Remembering this was an Earthling, I pointed out to him. "One of the reasons the Golden Halo is so popular is it assures the passengers, especially on this level, complete privacy. You may not be aware that some come on board to...to what is the correct word?"

"To have affairs?" The Earthling asked with a deep sigh while shaking his head.

"Affairs?" I asked, knowing the word but needing help understanding the context of this conversation.

"Ah, ah," He stammered, seeing my confusion. Finally, he said. "Oh, trump. Passengers come aboard to have sexual relations that they don't want to be made public."

"Yes, that's it," I said with a smile, not understanding why he was embarrassed by saying this. "So that is what an affair is? Fascinating. What was that other word you used?"

"Ha, an old Earth curse word. I apologize for using it in your presence."

"What does it mean?"

"A long story. Just don't use it in public. You are sure to offend someone. Ah, ah, and a princess can't have that."

"I offend people all the time. Is this like the word that starts with an F? As a child, I said it once, and my mother made it clear to never say that vulgar word again."

"Worse." The Earthling said with a smile.

After much debate and a call to Lady Venusun, the Earthling finally moved closer to the weapon and knelt down. He didn't touch the gun, but he was closely examining it. "I haven't seen a gun like this for years."

"What kind of...you called it a gun?" I asked, kneeling down beside him, tugging down my too-short dress. The Earthling noticed this and smiled.

"Ah, for our next murder, you will have to wear pants," he said and then seemed to immediately regret it. "Sorry, that's what we call cop humor back on Earth."

"I wasn't offended. It was an excellent suggestion. I could go get your bag and change at the same time."

"I would be very grateful for that," he said with another smile. "Ah, ah, for getting my bag. You don't have to change," he said.

"Of course I do. This dress is ruined. I do thank you for pushing me to the floor and apparently saving me from physical harm, perhaps even death. I need to change because the little voice in my head tells me tonight's events are not done."

"Ah, ah, sadly, I think your little voice is right."

I dashed as well as I could in spike-heeled boots to my cabin and quickly changed into pants called Levis, a shirt with the word Nike across the front, and very comfortable shoes with the same name on them. The last touch was a black cap. After this, I went back to Captain Zana's cabin. Thankfully, the body there had been removed. I retrieved the black case and rushed back to the crime scene much faster, thanks to the shoes I knew were called sneakers. They would be excellent for sneaking up on someone.

The hallway was clear except for the captain, ensign, and two crewmen holding a stretcher. They all looked anxious. I suspect they wanted to get the body out of sight as quickly as possible. Fross nodded to the bar.

The Earthling was bent over the dead doctor, avoiding the bloody wound. He was taking things out of the doctor's pockets. I stood a short distance away. "Is that really necessary? We know how the doctor died."

"Ah, yes, princess, that is quite obvious." The Earthling said, getting up and putting a money card and door card on the table. "I was hoping to find a clue. We need to find the other Earthling."

"Yes, we do," I said, thinking this was obvious. "The other Earthling did kill the doctor."

"Oh yes, that I am sure of. That gun is a Smith and Wesson Magnum 44. A very powerful Earth gun. It hasn't been made for centuries. This is a weapon that was handed down over the centuries. It must have been difficult for them to just leave it."

"Why would you think that?"

"The gun looks almost new. It has been oiled and cleaned by someone who cared about it. This murder was an act of desperation."

"I should say so. Shooting someone right in front of us? That is desperate."

"I would be more curious to know how they got it on board. They check everyone's baggage."

"Not mine," I said, a little shocked. "No one would dare touch my luggage. If anyone did, they would regret it."

"That's right," he said, pulling on his ear and smiling. You have what we call diplomatic immunity on Earth."

"Diplomatic what?"

"Ah, ah. No one is allowed to search your bags. So, it could be the Prime Centurion who brought it on board. Risky. Still, why bring this weapon? It would be too loud to use to kill her majesty."

"Unless they planned on blaming you. But that is ridiculous." I said with a smile. "They would have to know you were on board. Not even I knew you were on board..."

"No, no, you may be right." He said, stroking his chin while looking right at me. I was about to point out his rudeness for not only interrupting me, but now he was staring at me. Then I realized he wasn't looking at me. He was looking over my shoulder. The Earthling stood and smiled. "Ah, ah, Ensign Sig, a quick word, please."

I thought the ensign would run off because she looked over her shoulder, but the other crewmen were in her way. Then, she probably realized there was no place to run to. She took a breath, even I could hear, before slowing walking into the bar. I watched in disbelief as the Earthling put his arm around her shoulder and moved to the corner. I was definitely going to speak to the Earthlings about what is acceptable in civilized society, but that was for another time.

Naturally, I joined them. The Earthling was about to protest but must have remembered I was a princess. Then, he spoke in a whisper so quiet I could barely hear him. But the words made me think I had misunderstood him.

"Ah, ah, Ensign, this is between you and me," he said, looking at me. And Princess Deela. If you would be so kind as to tell me, Ensign: was it your mother or father who was from Earth?"

CHAPTER 36

ENSIGN SIG'S STORY

"How dare you accuse me of such a thing?" Ensign Sig said, sounding outraged. I would have been if I was her, except I would have slapped the Earthling. This young officer, an Earthling? One look at her pointed ears showed how wrong the Earthling was.

We all make mistakes.

Then I realized that I was showing my prejudice against Earthlings by agreeing with the ensign. This made me stop and think. I could feel my pink eyes spread into wide ovals. My jaw dropped a bit. Then, the tiny voice in my head started to laugh.

No. I was better than that. Feeling like I was in a dream. I watched the ensign start to turn away.

"I'm leaving." She said and started to walk away.

"Ah, ensign, do you really want me to call Lady Venusun?" He said in a louder voice, not moving. "One call…"

Sig whirled around. She was still angry, but this quickly faded. Fear filled her face. She rushed up to the Earthling and actually grabbed his arm and whimpered. "Don't. You will ruin my life. You must understand?"

"I do understand. Ah, ah, and I have no problem with what you are doing. These are hard times for anyone who has a connection with Earth. But there have been three murders. Murders that you or I were to be blamed for. This is the only reason I ask."

"I have nothing to do with those. I didn't even know them." She said, almost crying. "If the captain finds out."

"Ah, ah, Ensign Sig, by now, Lady Venusun probably knows your secret." He said, moving closer. "After finding out the ship doctor was not someone she would have hired, she is checking the backgrounds of the entire crew. Trust me, she won't care. But she will care if you don't help me."

"I don't know anything." She said with pleading eyes.

"Ah, ah, I think you do but are unaware of it. I am guessing your mother was from Earth?"

"Yes."

"Ah hmp, was she on Earth?"

"Yes, she is dead. I haven't seen Father for years." She abruptly stopped and looked down.

"Until tonight?" He asked.

"I am not sure it was him. He looked something like my father, but not really. Something about his eyes and the jaw. I couldn't be sure."

"That's why you fumbled the shuffle," I said, remembering how she dropped the cards. "The cards flew across the table. When that friend of the Prime Centurion came in and sat down. What was his name? Yes, yes, Daris!"

"That is not his name. His real name is Titalus. Before the war, he was a businessman. Mom said he worked with the Earthlings. Actually, more than that. He helped them take over his planet. She took me back to Earth when it was obvious the war was going against the Earthlings. I haven't seen him since. I only survived because my mother sent me to live with some of my father's family. Having these ears on Earth was difficult."

"How did you end up on the Golden Halo?" The Earthling asked.

"That's the odd thing." She said. "After the war, I applied to several companies for a position. I was surprised when this position was offered."

"Because you didn't remember applying?"

"Yes, but I couldn't turn it down. The money is too good, and there is the pension."

"Last question." The Earthling said. "Did you tell anyone I was on board?"

"No, I didn't know you...I mean, an Earthling was on board."

"Ah, ah, but you did know a mysterious passenger was on board. Staying in Lady Venusun's private suite."

"Everyone on the crew knew someone was in the suite. But who would have guessed it would be an Earthling?"

"Who, indeed?"

CHAPTER 37

THE EARTHLING PONDERS

"Thank you, Ensign," the Earthling said with a smile. You may go, and I will speak to Lady Venusun. Stop worrying about your position...and secret. As you can see, the lady will not hold this against you."

"How did you know?" Sig asked with anxious eyes.

"I wasn't sure until I got a closer look. You have your father's ears, but I suspect you have your mother's eyes. Your father's people don't have blue eyes. And just a feeling. There are so few Earthlings around. My radar is always looking for another Earthling. Many like you have taken to using disguises to avoid trouble."

"I should get contacts." She muttered.

"Ah, ah, that would be a shame. Your eyes are beautiful."

The ensign just shook her head and walked off. I watched her walk off and then asked. "What is radar?"

"Princess, if you would give me a moment." He said. "I need to collect my thoughts and the facts of the case."

At this point, he leaned back against the wall and closed his eyes. He brought up his hands and began to tap his fingertips together. A moment later, he began to hum that song again. After a few more moments, I felt foolish standing there. I started to look around.

"I think I have it." The Earthling said, opening his eyes and looking down at the doctor's body. "Ah, ah, I pray I am wrong. We have to search the doctor's cabin. Then, a word with the ensign's father. Perhaps a word with the queen. No, I can't put it off. One last person to chat with."

"The mysterious stranger!" I said a little too excitedly.

"The stranger. Why thank you, your highness." He said with a bow. "I had forgotten all about him. I suspect that is what he counts on; people do not notice him, but even if they do, they forget about him.

Yes, we must have a word with him. He might be dangerous if I am right in my assumptions, but I can't be wrong."

"So you know who the murderer is?"

"Not exactly. I know who pulled the trigger. Ah, ah, remember princess. The original plan was for the imposters to save the planet Earth. Noble cause with the best intentions, but more is needed to justify their actions. Back on Earth, they would say they were doing all this for the greater good. The plan to save Earth supposedly failed."

"Supposedly?" I asked, now confused.

"Ah, ah, no. This is too terrible to consider. Why? Why? Why would they want the Prime Centurion and Beta Chief to fail? They wanted to keep them in place. To continue the charade. But killing the queen really doesn't achieve anything. Unless the death of the queen was their goal all along."

"But why would this person kill the Prime Centurion and Optio?"

"This person didn't. There are two murderers. The poisonings ruined the original plan. The imposter's plan was to kill Queen Rexannis with that pistol. An Earth weapon. Once it was discovered there was an Earthling on board, I would be accused and probably convicted."

"But you never left your cabin." I protested. "There would be no evidence."

"Evidence wouldn't be needed. Very little would be needed. An Earth weapon and I would be enough for the public. The Prime Centurion and Beta Chief would have also pointed fingers at me. The final nail would be discovering one of the crew members was half Earthling. Easy enough to say we were working together. That would explain how I got the weapon on board."

"That is insane."

"Ah, your highness, you are a princess and above reproach. Very few people would accuse you of anything. Earthlings are accused of everything."

"Lady Venusun would come to your aid."

"Most likely, or I would hope so. It wouldn't be important that I be arrested and convicted in court. All they would need is for the media to convict me in the public's eye. All they needed was suspicion. With an Earthling around, who would suspect the Prime Centurion and Optio? While the true mastermind stays in the shadows. Completely unnoticed."

"Shocking." I gasped, thinking this couldn't be true. Then I recalled that not just minutes ago, I was horrified when he accused the ensign of being half-Earthling. Oh, I couldn't forget how Prime Minister Tunga treated him. I shook my head, looking at the Earthling. "Unbelievable, but I am sad to say it probably would have worked."

"You know how those Earthlings are. You just can't trust them."

"I desperately need a drink," I said, slumping against the wall.

"You can take the body," the Earthling called to the Captain and crew members. Clean this mess up. Princess Deela needs a drink."

CHAPTER 38

"Shouldn't you be searching for clues?" I asked, watching Fross happily give orders to remove the body and start cleaning this up.

"Let's get you that drink," he said, almost taking my elbow but then thinking better of it.

I smiled and said. "It would be most helpful if you gave me some support. I do feel a little weak in the knees."

"Ah, ah, are you sure?" he asked, but he took my elbow when I offered it. His touch was light but firm. In no time, he had escorted me up to the executive deck and into the parlor, where my favorite bartender was waiting.

I must mention the sight of the Earthling and me walking side by side, which raised a few eyebrows and even loud snorts of disapproval.

On any other day, I would have...have done what?

"The princess will have Daiquiri." The Earthling said. "Is it possible to make it a banana Daiquiri?"

"Of course...sir," the bartender said, then looked a little ashamed; he smiled at the Earthling and said, "This is the Golden Halo. Would you care for a drink, sir?"

"Yes, but I doubt you would know the drink, let alone how to make it," the Earthling said. I will take a beer."

"With all due respect, sir, I bet not only do I know your drink, but I can make it."

"It is called a Tequila Sunrise."

"A Tequila Sunrise. You should have ordered that for the princess. I suspect she would love the colors."

"Colors?" I asked, enjoying the small talk. For a while, there was no talk of murder.

"It is a beautiful drink." The bartender said, starting to busy himself behind the bar. "I think I will make two, and if Her Highness still wants the Daiquiri-"

"No, no. I like pretty and alcohol. It sounds like my kind of drink."

Faster than I could have believed, the bartender placed two tall glasses on the bar. They weren't just pretty; they were beautiful. This fantastic drink started out red at the bottom, slowly turning into a bright yellow. A cherry floated at the top. A tall red straw was stuck into the glass. I picked up the glass with a smile and then sipped. It was delicious. I took several more sips.

"Careful, Your Highness." The bartender said. "Those are like Long Island Iced Teas. They will sneak up on you."

"Sadly, my friend and I have work to do. So it will be the one drink." I noticed the Earthling had removed the straw from his drink and sipped it. "Without the straw? You are no fun."

"Ah, allow me to change your opinion in that matter." The Earthling said, taking out the cherry and eating it, leaving the stem. He held it up and put it into his mouth. It looked like he was going to eat it.

"You eat the stems of cherries?" I asked, but he held his hand while his jaw twisted around it. Then, just as quickly, he smiled. He carefully took the cherry stem out of his mouth. It was tied into a knot. I laughed too loud, making some people turn their heads, but I didn't care. "Why, you are full of tricks."

"Before I got married, I used that trick to pick up girls in bars," he said, his expression a little sad.

"Pick up girls in bars?" I asked and then realized what he was saying. "Oh, I see; you used that to meet girls. Oh yes, that would have caught my attention."

"Simpler times." He said, taking a long sip of his drink.

"That song, you hum. What is it?

"It was a silly song my wife used to sing. It is called A Brand New Key. I am trying to remember the singer. The chorus was something about her having a brand new pair of roller skates and the man she liked having a key."

"Sounds silly. I know what roller skates are. I have a pair. I am very good on them."

"I have no doubt of that, your highness. The one line in the song my wife liked was, 'Some people say I have done all right for a girl.'"

"I like that line too. Not to tell you your job, but the captain is cleaning up all evidence of the crime."

"If this turns out the way I think it will, Lady Venusun and Queen Rexannis will insist that all evidence of the crimes be erased."

"Why?"

"Right now, it best to keep my ideas to myself. Are you ready to continue with the investigation?"

I finished my drink and nodded. "Yes. You appear to have some kind of accent."

"Yes, you have a good ear. I was born in a country called South Africa."

"Oh, sorry, I don't know that one. Where are we going?"

"First to the doctor's cabin and then to have a word with the ensign's father or maybe your mysterious friend. Yes, let's see if the captain can put a name to this stranger."

CHAPTER 39

THE MISSING CASE

The Earthling searched the doctor's cabin, and I took notes while Fross tried to find out the stranger's name and what cabin he was in.

"It looks like the doctor was what we called a clotheshorse back on Earth," the Earthling said as he looked through the doctor's closet. Your Highness, are these suits in style? I can see they are well-tailored and expensive."

"Oh, I know what that means. A clothes horse is someone who has lots of clothes. That would make me a clothes horse." I moved over by the closet, stepping over the debris on the floor. As for the doctor, he lived like a pig. At least the captain kept his mess in the bedroom. Both rooms in the cabin were unmade. Not only were there clothes on the floor, but empty bottles. There were more empty bottles and glasses on the tables. The rumors about the doctor's drinking were more than true. I managed to make my way to the closet and studied the suits. I reached in and pulled one out. "This is a very nice suit. It is one of those suits that never really go out of style. I know this tailor. He is quite expensive. I wonder how a ship's doctor could afford it. These are all very much in fashion."

"Ah, first, your Highness, you are not a clothes horse. You are a princess. There is a big difference," he said with a smile. "Secondly, you are right. A ship's doctor couldn't afford these kinds of clothes."

"Whoever helped the doctor buy these clothes obviously got him the job on this ship."

He looked right into my eyes and smiled. "You are right, princess. The question is, why did they need the doctor on board? I understand putting the ensign here, but why a doctor? An ensign could go unnoticed by my employer but the ship's doctor. It was only a matter of time."

At this point, the Earthling dropped to his knees and began to study the closet floor. He rubbed his hand over it. I joined him on the floor and studied the carpet. I had seen this mark in many of the closets I used at home and on my travels. "There was a case here."

"A small one, but you are right." He said without looking up. "Probably a doctor's bag. Why would someone take his bag?"

"Maybe the murderer took it? There might be a clue inside that would reveal who the murderer is."

"Maybe," he said, sitting back, then tugging on his ear. Once again, he thought for a moment. This time, I waited. "Hmm, let's go talk to your stranger."

"If the captain has found out who he was."

CHAPTER 40

MY STRANGER

My stranger's name was Zumo Zecke. I pointed out to the Earthling that this was a common name on several planets. He told me this was interesting but wasn't surprised.

Then he looked at me with a grave face. "Ah, your Highness, I appreciate your comments, but I have to insist on this one. Please remain silent. I told you I worked in intelligence during the war. Yes, I was a spy. If this man is who I suspect he is, he was a spy, but of a different kind. I gathered information. He was an assassin. The man I know is very dangerous. He is very clever but also very dangerous.

"You mean this man murdered people during the war?" I asked in disbelief.

"Ah, ah, you don't murder during a war. You kill. At least, most of the time, you kill. That aside, if this man is here, he might have been hired to kill someone. So please, let me do the talking."

"Of course," I said, remembering an Earth phrase. "I will be quiet as a mouse."

"Well said, your highness." He said with that slight smile.

Mr. Zecke seemed to be waiting for us in his too-small cabin. It was one room with the bed taking up most of the space. A desk and drawers were built right into the walls. There was a chair for the desk and one tiny sofa. A window gave him a small view of the stars and planets. The room was exceptionally clean. As a matter of fact, it looked like the maid had just cleaned it. All the surfaces seemed to gleam. The man was sitting on the sofa, wearing the same plain brown suit. I now saw it was nicely pressed and well-tailored.

He did call out that the door was open when the Earthling knocked. Aside from that rudeness, he rose to his feet and bowed when I entered. He offered seats and drinks, both of which were declined.

After this, he sat down and studied the Earthling, who showed little interest. The tiniest of smiles came to his thin lips. "We both know you are not the first Earthling I have met. You might be one of the most interesting. I am pleased to see you made it through the war. I suppose you have guessed I have been discreetly following your investigation. Playing the same game. Letting everyone think you are not very clever. It worked well for you during the war. But we both know you are almost always the smartest person in the room."

"Ah, ah, well, sir, that is very kind of you to say, but Lady Venusun is much smarter than I. I am beginning to suspect the princess is, too," the Earthling said, not looking at me.

Which was good. I blushed at the Earthling's compliment but didn't believe him for a minute.

"Ah, ah, sir, let's just be honest with each other." The Earthling said with an amiable tone. "You may be interested to know the ship is now heading for Sirona."

"I suspected we have changed course. You think this changes things for me?"

"Yes, sir, I think it does. I think you were hired to kill Queen Rexannis. Before you object. The Queen isn't dead. So far as I can tell, you haven't broken any laws."

"You don't suspect me of all these murders?" He asked, leaning forward and putting his elbows on his knees.

"Definitely not the doctor. That was sloppy. Very unprofessional. The other two murders were very well planned. Someone put a lot of thought into them, but they just don't feel like you. I have seen your work. I suspect you were hired by the Prime Centurion."

"Without admitting to anything, I will just say the Prime Centurion and I had a business arrangement."

"Thank you, I understand. Ah, ah, so with the Prime Centurion dead, will you enjoy the rest of the voyage?"

"That was always my plan. I should mention something. I am doing this because I don't want Lady Venusun to become annoyed with me."

"Ah, ah, well, sir. With all due respect, you were going to do some work on her Golden Halo. She would be more than annoyed. This ship is the pride of her fleet."

"Exactly. This may surprise you, but I had learned the lady owned this vessel a day sooner. I wouldn't be here. Once aboard, I realized this and had second thoughts. I was going to give the Prime Centurion his fee back, but..."

"He died," I said out loud.

"Yes, he did," Zumo said, smiling at me. Then he returned his attention to the Earthling. "The Prime Centurion had a...what is the word. Oh yes, he had a boss. Sadly, I have no idea who this person is. But the Prime Centurion was afraid of him."

"Him?" The Earthling said, now more interested. "You think his boss was a man."

"That is the impression I got." Then he leaned even closer. "You seem to have some sway with Lady Venusun. If you could convince her that I have no intention but to enjoy the rest of this cruise, I would like to get off as quickly as possible."

"The next time I speak to Lady Venusun, I will mention that. I wouldn't be surprised if she, too, wants you off her ship as quickly as possible."

"Not her kind of person." He said with a small laugh. "Yesterday, I would have said the same thing about you."

"Ah, ah, well, sir, things change."

"Oh, one last detail, the now deceased doctor was brought on board to be part of this...what is the correct Earth word? Oh yes, conspiracy. I don't know what part he was to play, but it was important."

"Then killing him was an unplanned act."

"Exactly. They may be doing what you Earthlings called tying up some loose ends."

CHAPTER 41

After we left Zumo's cabin, the Earthling explained what tying up loose ends meant. We debated our next move when Queen Rexannis appeared in the passage and started looking out the transparent wall, studying the universe. She glanced at us.

The Earthling took this as a sign to approach. We walked up and waited. I noticed two guards standing at a discreet distance who appeared to be waiting for something to happen. The Queen was still dressed in black with a veil but wore a blouse with loose pants. It was more of an outfit one wore inside the palace, not generally in public.

"I do find space travel tedious." Queen Rexannis said without looking at us. "Now sailing on the water. That I enjoy. I have several boats."

"Ah, I am not a fan of small boats on water." The Earthling said. "I never quite got my sea legs."

When the Queen turned and smiled at him, I was about to ask what the Earthling was talking about. "You suffer from what is called seasickness?"

"Only on tiny boats."

"Then you wouldn't have that problem on my vessels. They are all quite big. I have been led to believe you suspect Bacco of smuggling a weapon called a gun onto the Golden Halo."

"Ah, ah, it is just a theory." He said. "I hope I haven't offended Your Majesty."

"I took no offense. But I did look through the Prime Centurion's things." She said, reaching into her pants pockets and pulling out two things. One was a much smaller pistol than the one used to kill the doctor. It didn't have the spinning cylinder to hold bullets. The other was a short, round metal tube.

"What is that?" I asked, moving closer.

Once again, the Earthling quickly took several steps back and put his hands behind his back. It was then I noticed the two guards had moved closer. For a moment, everyone just stared at each other.

"Queen Rexannis, it is illegal for an Earthling to even be this close to a weapon. Let alone touch it." The Earthling said, stepping even further back.

"I was led to believe you touched a pistol earlier in the evening?" She said with a smile. The two guards moved closer.

"I never touched the gun on the floor." He said, glancing at me. "Princess Deela will testify to that, and there are more witnesses who can confirm that fact. Since a murder had just been committed, I was legally safe to make sure the gun was turned over to the proper authorities. In this case, it was the captain."

"I was there. Captain Fross took the gun. The Earthling never touched it." I snapped, moving closer to the Queen and putting my hands on my hips. "You may be a queen, but I am a princess. I may not be the brightest princess, but I can tell when someone with a crown tries to get someone of lower status in trouble."

Another staring contest.

Finally, the Queen just smiled at me while she held out the pistol and whatever the other thing was. A guard came up and took them. Then, he carefully laid them on the deck. Queen Rexannis and her two guards started to leave.

"Ah, ah, you found these among the Prime Centurion's things?' The Earthling asked, making her stop.

She studied him for a moment. "I apologize for underestimating you. Now I see I am the fool in this matter. Rather, it was a new experience for me. I don't like it. My man will stand with the weapon until you get the captain here to pick it up. Earthling, am I your friend?"

"Ah, ah, Your Majesty, how can an Earthling be a queen's friend."

"I will take that as a yes," Rexannis said in a lovely tone. "You are very clever. I hope you find the murderer. I shall be in my cabin if you require my assistance."

"You have been more than helpful." He said and bowed. Too low for my liking. "Your majesty."

CHAPTER 42

THE ENSIGN'S FATHER

"What was all that about?" I said, following the Earthling away from the guard and the weapon. He was putting as much distance between him and it as possible. "I mean, Lady Venusun would have been outraged. She wouldn't have allowed you to be arrested."

"It wasn't about me being arrested." The Earthling said, stopping at the end of the passage. A steward came out of the parlor.

"Sir, Queen Rexannis just told me my assistance was needed here." He said. He looked nervous and seemed to be forcing himself to be polite. Lady Venusun's threat of losing his job probably filled his head.

"Notify the captain there is another pistol and a silencer down that passage. Queen Rexannis found them in Prime Centurion Uxtel's cabin. For obvious reasons, I can't be left alone with the weapon."

The steward nodded and touched the silver pin on his white jacket. This is called the captain.

Resolving the pistol and silencer issues took longer than expected. Finally, the guard confirmed our story, but only after Fross got frustrated and announced he would call Lady Venusun.

The Earthling and I could continue our investigation with the pistol and silencer taken away to be locked up in the ship's safe. For some reason, he had decided to seek out Ensign Sig's father.

"So that silencer thing makes a gun quiet?" I asked as we walked down to the last cabin. It was not one of the bigger cabins but was still on the executive level.

"Not completely. It makes a gunshot sound more like a thud," the Earthling said. The pistol itself was a Walter PPK. Centuries ago, it was a popular weapon with spies because of its size and weight. This brings up the question: Why not use that to kill the doctor?"

"Yes, a soft thud would be almost unnoticeable." I agreed, remembering the gunshot had left my ear ringing. Then I remembered how this all started. "You said the queen didn't want you arrested?"

"Ah, ah, no. The Queen was reminding me of my place. Reminding me she was a queen and that I was an Earthling. Quite unnecessary. It is impossible to forget my place in the universe at this time."

We came to the door. The Earthling politely knocked.

No answer.

Then he knocked harder.

Still waiting for an answer.

Then he banged on the door with his fist and said in a harsh tone. "Daris, don't make me get the captain to open this door. You are only making the situation worse."

Finally, the door opened a crack. The man I knew from the poker game peeked out. "What do you want, Earthling?"

"He wants you to open the door and let us in." I snapped, moving in front of the Earthling. "We are investigating a murder, and I suggest you open the door...Now!"

The man named Daris looked terrified but still hadn't opened the door. This man was forgetting his place, so I hit the door just as hard as the Earthling.

I was shocked. The man still didn't open the door. Now, not only feeling insulted but angry, I was about to shove my way in. Did this man not recognize my authority? Apparently, he finally realized who he was dealing with. The door swung open. The short, slender man wore a bathrobe similar to the Earthling's, except it was a dull white. It appeared to need washing. He could have passed for an Earthling if not for the pointed ears. His hair had been black but was now mostly gray. His eyes were round and surrounded by worry lines. His lips were so thin they kept vanishing when he sucked on the lower one.

I stepped into the room with my nose in the air, giving the room a regal glance. The cabin itself was, indeed, small with its own bedroom.

It needed a dusting but was clean enough. I chose not to sit. I could see the corner of an unmade bed through the door. I didn't think we had woken the man up because a movie was playing on his room monitor. This caught my eye because there was no color. It was all black, white, and gray. The film itself was more confusing. There were men dressed in robes fighting other men with long, thin swords. They were speaking a language I didn't understand.

The Earthling moved in front of the monitor and watched for a moment. Then, he studied the control panel before hitting a button. A tiny gold disc came out. More looking around. He found a case for the disc and carefully put it inside. The Earthling turned and said. "Ah, sir, I have to ask where you found a copy of Seven Samurai. Oh, this set includes both the Western remakes. Very hard to find. I have only seen bits and pieces but have always wanted to see the whole movie. Well, let's be honest, at this point in time, I would be happy to see any Earth movie."

"Take it," Daris said, slumping onto a small sofa and looking down at his bare feet. He should also consider his incredible rudeness toward a princess.

"Oh, that is very generous." He continued waving his hand in the air. "Back when I was a police officer, this would have been considered a bribe. So I have to ask myself: Why would you want to bribe me?"

"Then don't take it. I really don't care."

"Now that is a lie," he said, examining the case containing the movies. You see, the princess and I already know some things about you. For one, we know the Prime Centurion invited you on this cruise. We also know you have a daughter working on this ship."

"That's a lie! If you are talking about that half-breed filth." He snarled, jumping to his feet. I was shocked by his outburst and use of that foul term. But considering his behavior so far, I shouldn't be surprised. "If she is making that claim, I shall sue..."

"Sue her?" The Earthling said, quickly cutting the man's threat off. "That is a very Earth thing to say. No, Daris or whatever your real name is. I suggest you treat the princess more respectfully by telling us the truth. Now, as I was saying. The Prime Centurion invited you..."

"Fine. I will be honest. First, that wasn't the Prime Centurion. It was an imposter. An Earthling just like you. I knew him back in my home world. He worked in one of your agencies. You know, the ones with three letters. Always acting so mysterious. What you Earthling called cloak and dagger stuff. Like no one knew what they were. As for being invited, I was blackmailed into coming here. You think I want to be on a ship owned by Lady Venusun?"

"You worked with Earthlings." He said, looking at the movie case again. A smile came to his lips. "I see you picked up a taste for things from Earth. I suspect it was because you married an Earthling. Now, why would the Prime Centurion want you here?"

"The girl is my daughter. I was supposed to confirm she was half-Earthling if needed. It wasn't until I was on board that I realized the plot. The last thing I needed was to be involved in a murder. A murder that involved an Earthling."

"So you were surprised when the Prime Centurion died?"

"Why do you think I left so quickly? Actually, after I got to my cabin, I realized. His dying got me off the hook. Another Earth phrase. I just had to hide inside my cabin until we got to Icakka. Then, sneak off the ship. I doubted anyone would notice, with a dead body and an Earthling on board."

"You have friends on Icakka?" The Earthling asked, still studying the front of the movie cover.

"A few."

"Did you know Optio Zana and Dr. Crag are dead? Both murdered."

"What? Both of them?" Daris said, looking up with genuine surprise. "Then you know he was an Earthling, too. Crag did surgery on both of them and a little on me. When the man was sober, he was a brilliant surgeon."

"Back on Earth, he would been called a high-functioning alcoholic. The doctor's job was done. Why was he here?"

"The impression I received was he was needed for more operations and something to do with injections."

This made the Earthling look up. He was lost in thought once again. This time, he was not ear-pulling but stroking his chin. Then he looked up. "More operations? This last Earthling, who is he?"

"I don't know. The Prime Centurian and Optio were my only contacts. I know whoever this Earthling was, he was rich and powerful back on Earth. We both know what that means."

"He could be a wanted man." The Earthling said.

"No, no, all Earthlings were pardoned," I said. "According to my father, they were given these pardons and let go. Not that there were many places for them to go."

"Not all Earthlings were pardoned." The Earthling said. "There is a secret list of names. These Earthlings, if they are alive, are wanted. They were the men and women who were behind everything."

"Everything?" I asked, a little confused.

"He's talking about politicians and the heads of corporations. The men and women pulling the strings. Deciding to treat the universe like they did their own planet. Instead of invading countries, they invaded worlds. Not with weapons at first. The wars came later. All to increase their profits."

"It is suspected that some of these people escaped the destruction of Earth." The Earthling said with a deep, sad sigh. "There is even a theory that they were behind it. Covering their tracks, so to speak."

"Are you saying some Earthlings may have helped in the destruction of your planet?" I said, wanting to fully understand his statement. "That is just evil."

"Evil?" He said, looking at me. "Yes, that is a good word for them. As far back as I can remember, these evil people knowingly polluted the air and water for money. Money they didn't even need. How pathetic is that? Helping put the final nail in the Earth's coffin is not a far reach. In their minds, the Earth was doomed anyway. They just helped finish the job to cover their tracks."

"Cover their tracks?" I asked.

"Their escape. No goes looking for a dead person."

"They knew about you," Daris said. They assumed you would be the perfect...what is the word?"

"Fall guy? Patsy? Someone to take the blame." The Earthling said, just shaking his head. "But the Prime Centurion dying changed all that."

"Yes, now I suspect the last Earthling just wants to get off this ship."

"Just like you. Then maybe not. Men like him don't like to lose. I would like to borrow this," the Earthling said, holding up the movie but then putting it on a coffee table. But you will need something to pass the time. Maybe another time."

"Please take it. I have others."

"I am just borrowing it. It will be returned."

Then we left with the movie.

CHAPTER 43

BOYS AND THEIR TOYS

"I need to get this to Lady Venusun," the Earthling said, holding the movie with his fingertips. "After I fingerprint this, Daris is not our murderer, but he is wanted for something. He was being blackmailed. He probably worked with the kind of man we are hunting."

"That's a crime?" I asked and realized the stupidity of my question. "Of course it is. I swear I sometimes worry about the way my brain works."

"Ah, ah, your brain works fine, your highness." He said and started to walk a little quicker. We made our way back down to that very dreary bar with the plastic fish and nets. Thankfully, the doctor's body was gone. The bar actually looked much cleaner. There was no bartender, but there was the Earthling's case.

"Pity the bar is closed," I said, looking over at the bar.

"This won't take long, princess." He said, opening his case and going through the same process of taking the fingerprints off the movie case. "It is a shame. I would really like to watch this movie. I have heard of Steve McQueen and Denzel Washington. They are supposed to be excellent actors."

"They were both in this movie?"

"The Seven Samurai was a Japanese film. That was a country back on Earth. It was remade into what we called a western."

"Oh, I know what that is. It's a movie where Earthlings ride around on animals and chase other animals with horns. They carried what you called guns, too, if I recall correctly."

"Yes, the remakes. There were two were called The Magnificent Seven."

"Why were they magnificent?"

"Ah, ah, how to explain that. Okay, the heroes were what we called gunfighters. They were people hired to fight battles. Samurai were the same. In this movie, these seven people defended this village for almost nothing. They were risking their lives because it was the right thing to do."

"Ah, honor. I understand that."

"There are two more deaths, and you are still free?"

We looked up as Prime Minister Tunga walked into the bar. Once again, her black dress with silver trim wonderfully accented her figure. She stood there while watching the Earthling. He ignored her while working on the case. I did not. I stood up and said with authority, "If you're accusing the Earthling of murder, I suggest you rethink that. We are very close to finding the murderer. I would wager we shall have him before the morning."

"I understand the ship's doctor was shot?" She said.

"Yes, and before you ask, it was an Earth weapon known as a gun. We think the Prime Centurion snuck it on board."

"A gun. Smuggled on board. It sounds like it is just the thing an Earthling would do. The Earthling males did like their guns. Boys and their toys."

"What?" I asked.

The Earthling looked up with a strange look on his face.

The prime minister's demeanor changed. The Earthling just stared at her. Then, ever so quietly, with a slight smile, he said. "Boys and their toys."

The lady whirled around and stormed out of the bar. The Earthling watched her go. After she left, the smile vanished. He looked down at the fingerprints. Once again, he walked over to the wall and leaned against it. His eyes closed, and he began to tap his fingertips together. This time, it was shorter. He looked at me.

"You know who the murderer is?"

"Yes, but I need to speak with Lady Venusun."

CHAPTER 44

THE LAST MEETING

Once again, I sat alone in the Earthling's suite while he went into the bedroom and talked to Lady Venusun. They were in there a very long time. I was deciding they were both being very rude when Queen Rexannis came into the suite without even knocking. She went straight into the bedroom without even acknowledging me.

Finally, the Earthling came out and smiled at me.

"Your Highness, please be patient," he said, bowing, which was entirely unnecessary considering we were partners in solving this murder. I will be right back."

"May I come along?" I asked, standing up.

The Earthling thought about this and finally nodded.

We left the suite, moved down the hallway, and went around a corner. The Earthling put his finger to his lips, which I knew was a signal to be quiet. I heard a door open. I couldn't help myself. I peeked around the corner and watched Prime Minister Tunga walk toward the Earthling's suite.

"Go let her in. I will join you in a few seconds." He said, moving toward the door.

"Where are you going?" I asked.

"Please, your Highness, I need you to make her think you have been summoned to the suite with her. Please, I beg you."

"Very well, since you asked so nicely, but you better explain yourself to me later in detail."

"Trust me. You will know everything. There will be no secrets between us. That was part of my agreement with Queen Rexannis and Lady Venusun."

"Oh, then I will speak to you soon," I said, then rushed down the hallway. I reached the prime minister just as she reached the door to the Earthling's suite. I smiled at her. "I see you have been summoned too."

"Yes, where is your friend from Earth?" She asked in a dry tone. "Still sticking his nose into places he shouldn't? Once we get to Icakka, I will formally complain against the Earthling, Lady Venusun, the Queen, and you."

"Good luck with that," I said, using an Earth saying I had picked up. Smiling, I opened the door.

"I see you are picking up some of his slang. I would think that a person of royal blood would know better."

We walked into the suite and found Queen Rexannis sitting quite at ease in one of the chairs, holding a glass of wine. She nodded to both of us. I nodded back and went in search of some wine for myself. Prime Minister Tunga stopped and almost walked out, but she thought better. She bowed to the Queen. "Your majesty, may I sit?"

"Please do," Rexannis said with another smile, looking very pleased with herself. "Have some wine if you wish. You may need it. You may sit too, Princess Deela. This won't take long, but we should be comfortable."

I found the wine and a glass just as the Earthling came in. He stopped to put something behind one of the sofas. Then, I moved to the center of the room. He bowed to the Queen and then me and then turned to the prime minister. "These murders are the result of a plot. A plot that started with the noblest of intentions. At least, I am sure the men impersonating Prime Centurion Bacco Uxtel and Optio Zana had the best intentions. They were trying to save the Earth."

"Pray tell me how they ever thought the Earth could be saved?" the prime minister said. They weren't part of the twenty. The Prime Centurion was there to give his opinion, and that was all. The cold, hard fact was that the fate of the Earth had already been decided."

"Actually, that is not true." Queen Rexannis said. "The fact was they were divided on the course of action. You may not know this, but I was asked to be part of the twenty. I refused to attend. But you did it against my wishes."

"The names of the twenty were supposed to be kept secret. No one was to know." The prime minister said, looking a little nervous.

"Ah, ah, I will come back to that." The Earthling said. "The fact is, for whatever reason, they failed. Now, the smart thing for these men to do would have just been to vanish. Questions would have been asked, but nothing more. Instead, they showed up in the Golden Halo with a desperate plan. They were going to assassinate the Queen and put the blame on me. Knowing my being Earthling might not be enough, they arranged, through bribery, to have Ensign Sig, who is half-Earthling, brought on board. They also blackmailed her father to come on board to point the finger at what many would consider his half-breed daughter. The final player was a man who I knew to be an assassin. We crossed paths during the war. All the players were in place. All that was needed was for the assassin to do his job."

CHAPTER 45

THE SOLUTION

"I suspect Her Majesty was to die at the beginning of the voyage." The Earthling continued.

"Why did they wait?" the prime minister asked, not looking very happy. She kept finagling with the hem of her too-short skirt.

I wanted to know this too, but as they say back on Earth, this was the Earthling's show. I raised my glass and realized I hadn't even poured wine. I corrected this at once and took my sip. I nodded my approval and made a note to ask Lady Venusun where she purchased it. The Earthling must have noticed me looking at the label and asked if I was all right. "I am enthralled. Pray continue."

Then I realized I should be taking notes and began to search my jacket pockets for the notepad.

"The assassin, a fellow I met during the war, was quite good at his job. More than capable of completing it. He was having doubts. I mean, who kills a passenger, a queen no less, on a ship owned by Lady Venusun? She is indeed a powerful woman. He was nervous about this. Princess Deela even saw him a few times on this level. This was a man who had a talent for not being noticed. I suspect some negotiations were going on. But then these all ended when the Prime Centurion was poisoned."

"So you are saying another person poisoned the Prime Centurion?" The prime minister asked with raised eyebrows. "Not the aforementioned Earthlings? I have my doubts."

"That became even more evident when Zana was killed with the same poison. Before he died, the Beta Chief mentioned a third Earthling on board. Another man. His appearance had also changed. Before he was shot, Dr. Crag said his work on this man was his masterpiece. I'd like to point out something that bothered me. Why was the doctor shot? Especially with a weapon that was so loud it could be heard all over the ship. I was even more confused when Her Majesty showed me a pistol with a silencer that would have been better suited for the murder."

"Please tell us why?" Ley said, looking quite confident. "You seem to have all the answers...Earthling."

"It was the only weapon available to him." The Earthling said. "The murderer didn't have access to the Prime Centurion's suite. So this man either brought it or got it out of the Optio's cabin. It doesn't matter. The murder of the doctor was an act of desperation. Maybe even panic. Dr. Crag knew who the third Earthling was, but the doctor had more operations to perform. Since the plot was falling apart, he had to die. Then, this man would just wait. Wait for another opportunity to kill the Queen."

"So this third Earthling is going to escape." I gasped. "The Queen's life is in danger. You must find him."

"I already have." The Earthling said, looking right at the prime minister. "I don't suppose you will save us the trouble by admitting it."

"How dare you accuse me?" Prime Minister Tunga growled, jumping to her feet. She tried to slap him, but he quickly caught her hand. I was shocked by his quickness and the fact that he was touching the prime minister. Then, adding to the problem, he smiled.

"The doctor made you look younger, but you are still an old man inside." The Earthling said. "You gave yourself away when you used the Earth phrase 'boys and their toys.' You realized your mistake and stormed out of the bar. Sadly for you, in your rage, you fell out of character. You walked out in a definite masculine manner. Oh yes, your perfume is not covering up the odor of your cigarettes. The Princess and I found a crushed-out cigarette. An Earth cigarette with lipstick on the tip. Real cigarettes from Earth cost a great deal of money."

"Lies, all lies." She snapped. "Oh, have your little moment Earthling. We will be at Icakka tomorrow. I am the prime minister. It will be my word against yours. Who will believe an Earthling?"

"Ah, ah, we have changed course. We are heading for Sirona at top speed. We should arrive there in two weeks. You will be confined to your cabin." He said, walking away and picking up a leather doctor's bag from behind the sofa. The Earthling smiled. "Hmp, you won't be getting your injections. I suspect your skin will no longer be green when we reach Sirona. I also took the liberty of taking the green hair dye from your suite. So whatever color your hair is will start to show."

For a few moments, she or he stood there in shock. I was shocked, too. Then, whoever this was glanced at the door and must have remembered we were on a spaceship. She pulled her arm away and glared at the Earthling.

"How could you betray your own kind?" She snarled. "This was our only chance."

"Ah, ah, no, it was your only chance." The Earthling said. "You were in a position to know the war was ending. You also knew if the Earth was spared, you would be one of the few people held accountable. You would be put on trial and most likely executed or imprisoned for life. I could understand you fleeing to escape, but then there is your nature. Your greedy nature. You just couldn't stand the idea of being a fugitive. Moving place to place, always looking over your shoulder. I suspect the moment the plan to replace the Prime Centurion and Beta Chief came to your attention, the wheels in your head started to spin. I now know Prime Minister Ley Tunga was among the twenty. As you said, the names were supposed to be kept secret. Her Majesty didn't want to be part of the final act. As she stated, you went against her wishes and actually volunteered."

The Earthling seemed to think for a moment and then asked. "Ah, ah, I am curious. How did you pull off the switch? The Prime Centurion and Optio had been captured. But the prime minister couldn't have been easy."

"So you don't have all the answers." The other Earthling said with a snort.

"It really doesn't matter, but I know this plan must have been formed at least a year before the war ended."

"More like two." I chipped in. "I had a friend who had a sex change operation. The outside is easy. The inside takes time. I don't know why I didn't spot it at first. I guess the doctor did have talent. Still, the people close to the prime minister would have noticed the change in her personality."

"Would they?" The Earthling asked.

"Probably not." Queen Rexannis said. "Like me, Ley had no family. Being prime minister, no one would question her authority."

"But she," The Earthling said and stopped. "He was going to ensure his safety and strengthen his hold on power on Icakka. You could give yourself the injections. Yet the doctor was here."

"Oh! Oh." I exclaimed. "He had more work for the doctor. He was going replace more Icakkaians with Earthlings!"

"In time, but there was another reason," the Earthling said, looking disgusted at the prime minister. I wish I was surprised, but I keep thinking of the old Earth saying: Power corrupts. Absolute power corrupts absolutely. Was there even a time when you thought of anyone but yourself?

The person I now knew was not only an Earthling but had been a man who began to yell a stream of words that sounded terrible. They appeared to have no effect on my friend. There was that lovely smile on his face. Finally, Ley finished. In a rather disgusting manner, she wiped spit from her lips with the sleeve of her dress. "Ah, ah, my mother kept telling me that swearing was an ignorant person's way of expressing themselves. It appears she was right."

"Be careful; the game is not over," Ley said with a smile.

"You are referring to your prisoners." The Earthling said. "I suspected that the Prime Centurian, the loyal captain, and Prime Minister were alive. You were smart enough to know you might still need them to keep the deception going. Lady Venesun has the best people. She was able to backtrack your travels. The law enforcement officials on the second moon of Titus found your people, arrested them, and the hostages have been rescued. All three are now on a ship. We should rendezvous with the ship in three days. Fortunately, my employer and Her Majesty had decided to keep this matter secret. We Earthlings have a hard enough time as it."

At this point, four of the Queen's guards came in and stood by the door. The Earthling glanced over and then back at the imposter. "I believe Queen Rexannis has several questions of her own for you. Your Majesty, she...he is yours."

"I knew we would be excellent friends from the moment we met." Queen Rexannis said, standing and finishing her wine. She motioned to the guards. "Take the prime minister back to her suite. She will be guarded until we reach home. I don't know who you are, but I promise you, in time, I will know."

The Queen walked over to the wet bar and put down her glass. She smiled at the Earthling. "Do you wish to know who he really is?"

"I have my suspicions, but it would be nice to have them confirmed."

At this point, the person everyone thought to be Prime Minister Tunga broke into tears as the guards escorted her out. She or he slumped, and they had to almost carry her or him out. The Queen stuck out her hand. The Earthling bowed and kissed it. Then, she said, "Clever fellow. I will have to remember that. I owe you a debt I cannot repay. You gave me back, my beloved. If I can ever be of assistance, contact me."

The Earthling bowed very low and said, "You owe me nothing. The reward is that you have been reunited with the man you love."

Then, the Earthling and I were left alone. I sipped my wine and studied the words the fake prime minister had yelled. I had written them down. He took a beer from behind the bar and took a long drink. "What do these words mean?"

"Those are words that a princess should not know," he said, reaching over and ripping the page out of the notebook.

"They are still up here. I will do some research." I said with a smile. Then, suddenly, I thought of something. "Wait a moment. The

Earthling killed the doctor. Who killed the Prime Centurion and Optio?"

"The queen, of course." He said. "I thought that would have been obvious. You know a woman scorned."

"I have no idea what that means."

CHAPTER 46

NOW WHAT?

"It means Queen Rexannis was not fooled for a moment, but she is a queen. As a princess, you know reputation is everything to one of royal blood."

"Not everyone," I said with a smile and sipped my wine. "Pray continue."

"Ah, princess, you are the exception to so many rules. You definitely walk your own path."

I thought about this for a second and giggled. "Yes, I do. You are stalling. Continue."

"It wasn't just her reputation she was concerned about. In her mind, these were the men who killed a man she loved. No, exposing them in public wouldn't be enough. She would have her revenge and avoid the embarrassment of a trial. I doubt she knew about the prime minister, but she knew her life was in jeopardy. So she struck first, not realizing she was foiling a bigger plot."

"Do you know how she did it? I mean, we know she used poison, but how did she get the poison into the glass?"

"My guess is she got a hold of some liquid cyanide and filled the glass with it. Then dumped out the contents and let it dry. The inside of the glass was still coated with the cyanide. She put the glass back into the case. The imposter filled the glass with whiskey and the poison mixed in."

"Oh, clever. Getting to the glass wasn't a problem. The Queen was his fiancé. Why didn't she do the same with Zana's glass?"

"She couldn't be sure what glass he would use, so the poison went into the bottle. After the Optio died, the prime minister knew his plot was falling apart. He panicked, got his own pistol, went down to the bar, shot the doctor, dropped the gun, and fled. He shouldn't have dropped the gun."

"Because the gun told you the killer was an Earthling."

"Obviously, we already suspected that."

"Oh yes, we were thinking the same thing," I said, taking another sip of wine. Then I realized there was going to be a trial. "Oh, by the Goddess, there will be a trial. It will all come out. Oh, a trial won't be good for you. Putting it delicately, you are an Earthling. Of course, my family won't be pleased. A princess in the middle of all these murders, with an Earthling no less. Oh, I am sorry!"

"Hmp, You weren't listening very carefully. No need to apologize." He said, then taking a long drink of beer. "There will be no trial. Once Queen Rexannis has her answers. The Earthling is lucky that Pirme Centurnie is alive. Her questioning would be more...Intense. The man will be lucky to be put into an airlock and blown into space."

"What? You agreed to this." I asked, looking into his face.

"Not only did he vote for the destruction of Earth. I suspect he influenced the other voters."

"I wonder why he became a woman."

"The prime minister was a woman. I understand most of the power on Icakka rests with the women. Ah, ah, and a woman can be more persuasive than men in some ways."

"Are you suggesting he used his new body to...Euuu!"

"Of course, there is always the chance he secretly wanted to be a woman. I doubt it because the doctor was supposed to turn him back into a man. I suspect the Prime Minister is wealthy. His plans had failed. He would steal as much as he could. Hopefully, it was enough to get the operation he wanted. Then he would vanish./

"Do you know who he really is?"

"The last president of Earth loved guns. I recall there being numerous pictures of him holding a Smith-Wesson 44. He claimed it was the original gun from some movie."

"With his wealth and power, he could have just vanished. Instead, he tried to take over another world."

"I am told power is very addictive. Never having any real power, I wouldn't know. And I don't think I want to know."

"So what happens to you now?"

"I am still working for Lady Venusun. Before all this happened, I was on my way to investigate a series of burglaries in Galis. The last break-in resulted in a death."

"So you go where Lady Venusun tells you to go and solve crimes."

"Yes, that is what she pays me for," the Earthling said. So, we will be going our separate ways.

"Mmm, yes, we will," I said, tapping my finger on the rim of my glass. I really needed a manicure. My eyes drifted to Earthling, who had moved away and was sitting on the sofa. I walked over and smiled. "No, I will speak to Lady Venusun about becoming your partner."

"What?"

For the first time, the Earthling looked surprised.